John A. B. Williams, George S Fobes

Leaves From a Trooper's Diary

John A. B. Williams, George S Fobes

Leaves From a Trooper's Diary

ISBN/EAN: 9783337009281

Printed in Europe, USA, Canada, Australia, Japan

Cover: Foto ©Andreas Hilbeck / pixelio.de

More available books at **www.hansebooks.com**

FROM

A Trooper's Diary.

PHILADELPHIA:

Published by the Author.

1869.

DEDICATED

To the Author's

Companions in Arms,

THE

"ANDERSON CAVALRY."

CONTENTS.

I.

THE CAMP OF '61.

YESTERDAY I took a stroll to the site of my first camp. It is not far from Girard College, and I found that the walls of the extending city had encroached somewhat upon the place. But there was the field, without doubt, looking as green and fresh as on that summer day, eight years ago, when first I entered it. The old house still stands under the ancient elms; the birds—could *they* be the same?—still flit and chirp among the leaves. The surroundings are quiet. No one lives in the house, apparently. There is nothing to tell the chance observer that this green slope was once bald and slippery with the wear of martial feet; that here a thousand men lived for two months in preparation for war.

Sitting awhile upon the fence, and musing, I had a new sense of the pleasures of memory. It required but little effort of the imagination to restore to this weedy field the well-worn paths, the rows of snowy tents, the throngs of bran-new soldiery. Nor were the stirring scenes outside of camp less vividly recalled.

Bull Run! where really for the first time in our war,

"Red Battle stamp'd his foot, and nations felt the shock."

It is the most singular field in history; from which the real victors fled, leaving the vanquished in wondering possession! The name will always be full of startling memories

to those who recall the gloomy days that followed the
battle, and the pale, stern faces that surged about the
news offices, as rumor followed rumor portentious and
bewildering. Hardly had the echoes of the contest died
away, ere we crowded to the recruiting offices and camps.
The merchant, the mechanic, the clerk, the student, gave
up home and all in a moment; and of these there were
not a few who trembled lest the surgeon's eye should detect
some physical disability which they would fain conceal.
The air was alive with the roll of drums, and the flag—
now dearer than ever before—fluttered in miniature from
every window, or floated its full folds from the house-tops.

Those were immortal days, when the hearts of the people
were stirring with the sublime purpose to save their threatened freedom, and—for the idea was even then gestating
—to share it with a bondaged race. Looking back now,
in the light of the present, it is impossible not to recognize
throughout that fearful struggle—from its beginning, thirty
years before the firing on Sumter—the hand of Him who

> "Sways the harmonious mystery of the universe,
> Even better than prime ministers."

But now, to get down from the fence. Here is the very
spot on which the Corporal and I put up our tent. The
pin-holes have long since disappeared, but there is still
the ditch that we dug, now overgrown with grass and weeds.
What hard, hot work it was, on that July day, to us soft
bodied clerks! How we panted and perspired, wandering
off at short intervals to the sutler's for beer, and more than
half repenting of our patriotism!

The first night brought also the first storm in camp.
What soldier does not recall it in his experience? I pulled
forth my diary—having brought it with me as an aid to
reflection—and read:

"Last night the clouds gathered heavily, and at midnight the rains descended and the floods came. I was awakened by the uproar, and arose in consternation. Found the Corporal already up and outside, securing the ropes and giving the pins an extra drive. The wind roared furiously, swaying and cracking the trees, and rocking our frail tenements to and fro like skiffs upon the sea. The rain was blown about in sheets, penetrated the tent, overflowed the shallow drain, and streamed under the canvas, floating away nearly all the straw of our beds. What remained was water-soaked, so that we could only squat despairingly on our heels until morning, thinking of the home comforts within a bow-shot of us. This morning we have fairly moated our castle, and may bid defiance to the next siege of the elements."

Next day we put on the livery of war. It is perspiring even now to think of those heavy, " re-inforced " trousers, the canvas-lined jackets, yellow-braided, and bobbed behind; the stiff, Puritan hat, with its handful of brass ornaments, which were affixed in various ways, as best suited the undisciplined taste of the wearer. As a rule the big men got the little clothes, and *vice versa* — a singular perversity, which, with the consequent swapping and trading, came at length to be looked upon as among the "customs of service." To those of us who were wont to be well dressed and who now expected lady friends to visit us in camp, it was a mortal struggle with pride to swathe our forms in this huge toggery.

We had sabres thrust into our hands the same evening, and the first dress parade was ordered — for the colonel was ambitious to see his growing regiment in line. It was a ludicrous array of swaddled heroes. Falstaff, I imagine, would have preferred to "march through Coventry" with his shirtless ragamuffins rather than have led our amply clothed battalion! There was much swearing at the Quartermaster, who in turn swore at the Arsenal authorities; but, upon the whole, the boys took it good-humoredly, and enjoyed the fun of the thing as much as the spéctators.

The first guard duty is a memorable event to the soldier. Here was my first "beat," along this fence. When the keen-looking sabre was belted around the jacket (the latter folded over back and front for the purpose), and the clank of the blade in the scabbard startled the recruit as he stepped off with martial tread, he felt then that he was indeed a defender of the flag. His bosom swelled almost enough to fill out the laps in his jacket. He was only puzzled to know what to do with his weapon: how the deuce to carry that scabbard so that it might not trip up his heels, or entangle itself in his legs. But O what misery in the long hours of tramp, tramp up and down a prescribed distance, in the hot sun, or in the rain and mud; in the incessant vigilance required to do homage to the officers, who *would* wander by, in blue and golden glory, to seek such salutation. And then at night the rudely broken slumber, the silent and seemingly endless hours, the intense straining through the darkness for the relief, and the informal reception of it when it came.

"Who's that?" shouts the hopeful guard.

"Corporal with the relief."

"Good! hurry up, for Heaven's sake," &c.

What matter if the Corporal takes him to task for it, or reports him to the sergeant? He is relieved—that is his happiness – and may rest for four hours. How sudden and sweet is the soldier's first sleep by the guard-house fire, after his maiden watch! Sweeter far than any after slumber; for with every day of service he learns to sleep less soundly, so that the slightest bugle-note or tap of drum rouses him at once to duty.

Crowds of visitors roamed through the camp, peeping into our new white tents, and regarding us curiously, as though we were already heroes of a hundred fights· Baskets of delicacies and bundles of notions were daily received by the fortunate ones whose friends or relatives were within easy distance. Few of us, indeed, except the Germans (of whom there were several companies in the command) were compelled during our stay here to feed on army rations; scarcely a tent but had its store of home-made dainties. But the frugal and adaptable Dutchmen took straightway to the food which the Government set before them. We natives affected at first to look down upon our comrades from Faderland as mere hirelings, who had apparently been newly imported as "food for powder;" but they soon proved themselves worthy descendants of the stock that marched and fought under Blucher and Schwartzenberg.

Over in that field the buglers used to practice. What a lamentable set of blowers they were! I remember how strange it seemed to me they could not do better, being Germans, to whom wind instruments come as naturally as do pretzels and beer. But it mattered little, then, how they rendered the calls: the notes fell upon ignorant ears. With every toot of the bugles, recurring with bewildering frequency, the recruits might be heard calling to each other in vain what *that* meant, while the more careful and conscientious sought their officers for information. probably with as little success.

Behind the house yonder stood the Colonel's quarters, I recall him vividly. A long, sinewy Dutchman, with hair and features after the irrepressible type of Israel. He wore great, baggy, white pantaloons, spurs, a blouse, and a little forage cap that was almost hidden in his crisp hair. He persisted in dragging at his heels on all occasions a

huge artillery sabre, which weapon, it was whispered, had
cut off a score or two of heads in the German wars. The
Colonel dashed into camp and out again, with much ado
a dozen times a day, followed by two or three orderlies.
His chief occupation during these visits seemed to be
swilling beer and smoking pipes with a few favorite subordinates. Once only he shambled down among the
native companies, but finding that his pompous military
airs evoked only amusement, he quickly withdrew, and
contented himself with holding special reviews of the
German companies, and making speeches to them in his
native language.

As an impartial historian, however, I am bound to add
that the Colonel was pleased—probably as a "sop to
Cerberus"—to promote me to the non-commissioned
staff as Commissary Sergeant. I again open my diary:

"As the Commissary is not yet appointed (the duties of
the position being performed by the Quarter-master), he
details me to act as his own secretary. He directs also that I
put off the cumbrous regimentals in which I presented
myself, and resume my civil garb, until a new uniform
can be obtained from my tailor. He seems to have a
weakness for a well-dressed staff, albeit shabby enough
himself. Perhaps it is the contrast he likes; it was so
with Napoleon and Frederic. The cost of this new suit,
he says, can be collected from Uncle Sam; but a diligent
search of the Regulations reveals to me no provisions for
such expenditure.

"However, I obey. There is no questioning the commands of an old soldier who has chopped off heads in the
German wars.   *   *   *   *   *

"My first duty as secretary was to write a flaming letter
to the Quartermaster-General, demanding that horses be
furnished this regiment immediately; receiving no reply

to which, I had much difficulty in dissuading the Colonel from a direct appeal to the President. * *

"The Commissary reports for duty. A most villainous looking Dutch Jew, with eyes like an alligator's. By order of the commander, I report at once to the new-comer who replies, softly and insinuatingly :

" 'I dells you vot you do—I dells you.'

"Thinking, therefore, that I was now relieved from duty at head-quarters, I took up my abode beside the Commissary's. Had not been moved fifteen minutes before the Colonel's sonorous accent was heard :

" 'Gommissary Sarchent! Vare ees dot Sarchent of de Gommissary?'

"I repaired forthwith to the presence. His brow and voice were savage.

" 'Sarchent! You haf go away mitout leaf.' I pleaded my office, and his own orders to report to the Commissary. My fault was too evidently one of ignorance, and his ruffled spirit grew serene.

" 'You must keep mit *me*,' he said, 'und let dot Gommissary sent for you !'

"Whereupon I mentally sent the Commissary to the devil, and renewed allegiance to the chief."

The summer weeks wore on. By and by the effect of discipline became apparent. The candidates for glory, having had their rotund garments skilfully tailored, and their faces bronzed by sunshine and storm, began to look like soldiers. The companies march like squads of automatons. The buglers wind their horns more musically, and every call is obeyed promptly and without question. The drills and parades are splendid sights, crowding these fields and fences with spectators.

At last, when camp life had grown so monotonous that the veriest skulker longed for activity, orders came to move.

2

The camp at once became a scene of uproar. Far into the night the Teutons yelled their songs of Faderland, the natives sang and fiddled national airs. Others scratched hasty notes to loved ones, or perchance stole out of camp for a farewell interview.

Alas! that four years' storm of woe—the falling of tears, the riving of hearts—had already burst upon thousands of homes.

What imagination can compass the accumulated grief that had settled down at the firesides of this people when they emerged once more into peace?

With the first gray of morning came the noise and confusion of tearing down and loading up, the braying of mules, the shouting of teamsters, the loud commands of excited officers. The regiment was formed with the left resting under that elm. Pockets, bundles, and haversacks were stuffed almost to bursting with the extra baggage bestowed by friends who meant to be kind. Cheer after cheer arose as the commander, resplendent in a new uniform, and soaked to the eyes in beer, dashed along the front, clanking with his spur the bloody sabre of the German wars, and followed by he of the alligator eyes and the full staff, including the "Sarchent of de Gommissary."

In the heat of a mid-summer morning we marched to the depot, whence the long train finally bore us away toward Washington, amid tears, and cheers, and smiles, and the waving of a thousand handkerchiefs.

It is only fair to add, as a sequel to these recollections, that the Government soon found it advisable to dispense with our commander and his sword, notwithstanding the latter's bloody record in the German wars!

II.

THE GUNS OF ANTIETAM.

OUR detatchment came down from Carlisle to Chambersburg, on the night of September 16th, 1862, and took up quarters in the stables of the Fair Grounds, about a mile from the town. I turned in with my bunk-fellow* on a bundle of old hay, and we slept soundly until hunger aroused us at day-break. We had brought three days' rations in our haversacks; but being still in "God's country," we chose rather to turn up our noses at such fare, and seek elsewhere a more substantial meal.

Putting ourselves, therefore, in as good trim as pocket-combs and glasses would permit, we shook out some of the dust from our regimentals, and started down the turnpike, with the design of stopping at the first inviting house. The east was glowing redly with the approaching sun; the morning air was dewy and sharp; the early bird twittered among the bushes by the roadside, or perched for an instant upon the top rail of the fence, to swallow the proverbial worm.

We passed several habitations that did not look inviting. One of them we approached, and my companion had laid his hand upon the latch of the gate, when a savage growl echoed from the rear of the premises. Presently a huge white bull-dog, of the most surly species, flew up to the

---

* Wilbur Watts, Burlington, N. J.

gate. But we were already some distance away, with an intuitive conviction that those people were not hospitable to the soldier.

The next house was small, and of the old yellow plaster style, embowered in vines and evergreens of a half century's growth. It looked attractive; but seeing no signs of life about the place, we would have passed it, had not there appeared from the recesses of a side porch an old man, leaning upon a cane, who beckoned us to approach. Only too glad to go, we were speedily beside him.

"You are soldiers, boys," said he; "I'm always glad to see our soldiers. I was once a soldier myself. Have you had breakfast? or are you now on some important duty?"

We assured the old gentleman that we could await breakfast without any neglect of duty. He seemed delighted, and led the way into the house, and would have put us forthwith into the parlor, but we persistently refused to invade its cleanliness and quiet.

We seated ourselves in the kitchen. The old gentleman disappeared for a few minutes, returning with a young girl whom he presented as his grand-daughter. She was a round little body, with blonde hair, and a sweet flushed face. The grandfather apologized for the absence of his son and daughter (the girl's parents), who were visiting friends at Gettysburg. While the grand-daughter bustled about for breakfast, we talked to the veteran, who had meanwhile lighted his pipe.

"You say you've been a soldier, Mr. Lyon—in 1812, I suppose?"

"Yes in '12. It's a long time ago, and I'm growing very old."

"How old, sir?"

"Past seventy-three."

"You bear it well, and bid fair to reach a century."

The old man shook his head.

"Ah, no!" said he, "I can never do that—never."

"I hope at least," I said, "that you will live to see these rebels whipped back into the Union."

He smiled and took a long whiff.

"Yes, I hope so, too, my dear boys, and I feel somehow. or other that I *will*. I wish I could help you, but I can only give you my blessing."

"Do you have a clear recollection of the scenes of *your* war?" asked Watts.

"Pretty clear, pretty clear," said the veteran.

We paused to give him an opportunity to narrate some of his experiences, and plied him with an additional question or two to draw him out; but he seemed disinclined to respond other than in monosyllables. Attributing his silence to modesty, or a desire not to be interrupted in the enjoyment of his pipe, we ceased to bother him.

Breakfast being ready, we sat down to and discussed it with a soldierly vigor that allowed of but little conversation. Neither the old man nor his daughter sat down to table with us: the latter kept herself busy replenishing our cups and plates, while the grandsire sat silently beside the window, puffing his pipe, and wondering, probably, at the extent of our appetites.   *   *   *   *

We had finished the meal, and were about to rise from the table (first taking care to conceal under our plates the bills which our host refused to accept), when a faint sound, like that of distant thunder, reached us. Watts and I knew at once what it was. I looked at the veteran. He was shaking the ashes from his pipe—evidently the sound did not reach him. Soon another rumble followed more distinct than the first.

"Do you hear that, Mr. Lyon?" I asked.

"Hear what, my son?"

"The sound of battle," I replied, rising and pointing to the South. The words electrified him.

"Why, no—you don't say that—really?" And the old soldier, bustling up from his chair, walked briskly to the door. Not hearing the sound immediately, we all went out with him to the gate.

And now, plainly enough, the roar of distant guns came up in a succession of subdued reports. The veteran heard it. His eyes kindled amid the embers of age. "Dear me," he said, stepping back and forth, and bending forward to listen, "it has been fifty years since I heard that. It carries me back to Plattsburg, where the sound almost deafened me. Thunder was nothing to it. Ah me! if I were only younger—only ten years younger— I'd put on my coat of '12, and take my old musket, and go forth again under the old flag. I would, boys, I would!" and the brave old fellow struck the ground emphatically with his cane.

Another burst of artillery, louder than any that had preceded it, seemed to arouse the old gentleman anew. "That's it! that's it!" he cried excitedly, "give 'em another like that; as we did at Plattsburg."

Turning to his daughter, who seemed rather apprehensive of the old man's excitement, he said quickly: "Run to the house, Anna—run girl, and bring me my coat and musket." Anna obeyed and the veteran continued: "I'm not so old, after all. I'll go with ye, boys! *Damn it, I'll go with ye!* I'll see the flash, and hear the musketry, anyhow."

He was pacing restlessly back and forth, striking the ground with his cane.

"I'm afraid we can't see it, father Lyon," I said; "our command is not yet mounted, and the battle will be over before we could reach the field."

"That's too bad," he said, "too bad. We needed every man at Plattsburg. Well, here's my coat—my coat of '12. Now you'll see the old man become a soldier again. Hurry, hurry, girl."

"Grandpapa," said Anna, as she approached with the coat, "your gun is too heavy for me to carry, so I left it."

"Ah! true, true," said her grandsire, "I was cruel to ask it of you. Perhaps I could not handle it myself."

She gave us a sly wink, as she said this, from which we inferred that other reasons had induced her to leave it.

"Never mind it; I'll put on my coat. Here,"—he said, giving me his cane, while Watts took his coat. The latter was of faded dark blue cloth, with worsted epaulets and trimmings, and metal buttons—a genuine old regimental. He was assisted to get into it—not a difficult operation, by any means, for it lapped over and hung loosely about his spare form. "Ah! boys," he said, "I used to fill this out roundly." Having buttoned his coat from chin to waist, we stepped off and removed our hats to the veteran. He appreciated the compliment, smiling with evident delight, and said:

"Come now, lads, I'll be your Captain—I'll lead you." He flourished his cane, and gave us some tactical commands, which we executed promptly, to his great delight.

All this while the thunder of the distant conflict was plainly audible, and the old soldier would relapse into silence every moment or two to listen. Then, supported on either side by a trooper, whom he entertained with voluble recollections of the past, this veteran of our second war of independence marched feebly but proudly up and down the path to the sound of his country's third life-struggle. The scene was sublime. Needless to say, our patriotism was newly and deeply stirred.

But we were already overdue at camp, and reluctantly hurried away. The good old man waved a farewell to us with his cane as far as he could see us. We did not expect to see him again; but as no marching orders came during the day, we ventured to return after nightfall, to tell him the news. The excitement of the morning had reacted upon the brave old fellow. We found him, helpless and feeble, stretched upon a settee.

But he was still enveloped in his coat of '12, and his eye grew bright again as we detailed to his wondering ear the first crude accounts of the great battle of Antietam: how Hooker was borne bleeding from the field—how Burnside's men stormed the bridge; and especially did we dwell in sadness upon the fall of our own brave young Stockton—the first mortal sacrifice which the cause had yet exacted from our command.

III.

ROUGH RIDING IN KENTUCKY.

A PLEASANTER five days' trip was never enjoyed than ours from Louisville to Bowling Green. The weather was delightful—those early winter days of the South, so full of sun-shine and breeze, and the clear frosty nights, that made double blankets agreeable.

Our regiment numbered nearly a thousand men, newly clothed, equipped, and mounted, and gloried in its strength. The ubiquitous Morgan was known to be skulking in the country adjacent to our line of march, and although his force was double ours, not a man of us but longed to fall in with the famous raider.

But we had not that pleasure. Morgan never fought unless he had every chance in his favor, and even then, as many of his bold troopers will acknowledge, he often got handsomely whipped.

We arrived at Bowling Green on the afternoon of a beautiful Sunday in December. Our camp was located on the grounds of a wealthy rebel in the southern edge of the town. The wealthy rebel was still at home enjoying his comforts, and, as it soon appeared, his privileges. For just as tin cups and regimental pots were simmering over the fires, up dashed an orderly, with a command from General William Sooy Smith, to vacate the premises forth-with. We were polluting soil which had been consecrated to the Confederacy. There was no help for it. It was then

3

the policy to make polite concessions to the rebels of local prominence as an acknowledgment of their chivalry. Especially was this so with certain young and lofty Brigadiers, to whom the favor of a rich rebel skinflint, or the treacherous smiles of his pretty daughter, were more welcome than the cheers of the soldiers. There was some "tall" swearing done by the boys when the order was promulgated. Major Rosengarten, in deference to their fierce expressions, delayed moving until morning, it being then nearly dark, and to search for and get settled into a new camp, would have taken us far into the night. The troopers blessed the Major; but, as it will appear, would have fared better if the move had been made at once.

Morning came and with it the breaking up. The sky was ominously leaden and heavy at daybreak, but no one thought of anything beyond a shower. Tents were soon down, wagons loaded and sent off, horses saddled. As we mounted the rain began to fall in big drops, and when we were got half way through the town, the flood-gates of Heaven opened upon us the most terrific rain-storm that I ever beheld. Faster and faster, heavier and heavier, it came, accompanied by blasts of wind that threatened to sweep both horses and men away. Rubber coats and talmas were of little avail. Bootlegs overflowed with water. The streets of the town became creeks and rapids; and when we had labored through them and got beyond the place, the prospect seemed more dreary and hopeless than ever. Slowly and wretchedly we toiled on through the flood and gusts, crossing swollen streams with the water over our stirrups, and the currents dangerously strong. Our poor animals were barely able to get along. We were to seek and occupy a camp in this storm! Where it was to be no one knew, not even the commanding officer. Hour after hour we labored on, and still the rain beat down. Would it *never* cease? In vain we glanced up from under our dripping visors to catch perchance some sign of a break in the dark sky. Al. Rihl grimly observed that something certainly was *broken* up there! The soldier's discomfort is seldom too great for a joke.

It must have been about the middle of the afternoon when our wagons loomed up dimly through the rain. Reaching the spot we found them up to the hubs in a field of mud. The tents and baggage had been unloaded and lay scarcely distinguishable in the mire.

"Is *this* our camping ground?" was the incredulous and indignant question.

The answer soon came in an order to dismount.

The Major now come in for a hearty cursing, as had the Brigadier before him. The boys thought it a pitiful exercise of judgment to select so palpable a mud-hole for a camp in a region where high, hard ground was plentiful.*

But we went sullenly to work. Night was fast approaching, and the rain—the relentless rain—still fell. It was long after night-fall when the last shelter was up. But our miseries were only intensified by the night. There was nothing to eat that was not soaked and sodden; no lights, no wood that would kindle. There was also but little food and less of other comfort for the horses, who pawed impatiently, often neighing piteously, all through the cold, drenching night, immersed half way to their knees in water.

There was nothing to do but to squat upon our saddles, shivering and doziug, while the water and mud ran in

---

*How mary soldiers of the Army of the Cumberland have explained to themselves this standing mystery: Why regimental and brigade commanders would so persistently and cruelly fix their camps and bivoucs—in dry weather, as remote as possible from wood and water: in wet weather, plumply in a mud-hole?

streams under us and over our feet. It was our first bitter experience in the field, and later ones were never worse. Scores of us were laid up in the hospitals for months, and some, alas, never came out of them alive.

Morning found us soaked and stiff, ravenous for nourishment. The storm had ceased, and a cold north-wind was crusting the liquid earth, and drying up the pools. In the distance, apparently not a mile away, were the spires and chimneys of Bowling Green, and nearer still we recognized the mansion of the wealthy rebel, whose land we had polluted. In our blind search for a camping ground, we had, it seemed, innocently marched in a circle around the town, halting at last near the original starting point! Of course this fact added greatly to our serenity and satisfaction.

We now transferred our effects once more a short distance nearer the town, on elevated ground thinly belted with cedars.

What a relief it was! How delicious was the odor of the coffee at breakfast, of the bean soup at dinner! The sunshine had never before seemed so lovely. The long lines of clothing which we hung up to dry, would have conveyed to a housewife the idea that ours was a camp of washerwomen. The poor beasts, too, were not forgotten. How they relished the corn and oats which we poured into their nosebags! My own little "Shiloh" frisked his tail and winked his big dark eyes with the pleasure of mastication.

But these comforts were not to continue long uninterrupted. In the midst of the coffee and hard-tack of supper, lo! a courier with more orders. The boys looked significantly at each other. Had we again unwittingly trampled upon sacred ground?

The courier (one of us) was stopped on his way out of camp, and informed us that John Morgan was at Glasgow, forty miles away, and that we were to make a night march thither to surprise him.

Those of us who were to go were, therefore, prepared for the order which soon came:

"Two days' rations, boots and saddles in half an hour."

We started, four hundred strong, at sunset.

"The moon was up—by heaven, a lovely eve!"

But it was also very cold, and the wetting which most of us got in crossing the Big Barron, rendered our ride doubly uncomfortable. The winds which had prevailed all day had measurably dried up the roads. We followed the Louisville pike for about ten miles, then turned eastward, crossing the Louisville and Nashville rail-road near Bristow's station. As we crossed the track the head-light of a locomotive was seen dwindling away in the southern darkness. It afterwards transpired that a freight train, bound North, had stopped at or near the station for some purpose, when the alert ear of the conductor caught the tramp of cavalry from the turnpike on his left. Believing that Morgan—who was daily looked for at all points of the line—was now really upon him, he reversed his engine and got away with all speed to Bowling Green. His scare was communicated to the garrison, which turned out *en masse* for the expected foe.

After several hours brisk riding, the road trending away nearly due south, we turned sharply to the east again into another road—and certainly one of the most extraordinary and uncomfortable by-ways ever traversed by mounted men.

Scarcely two yards in width, it led for many miles through forests so dense that not a ray of moonlight could penetrate them. The trees seemed twisted into all manner of shapes, and the limbs projected across the road at every angle. It was with the utmost difficulty that one could keep his seat. Hats were knocked off and scalps were grazed. The tall fellows caught it right and left, and several were fairly unhorsed. The guide at the head of the column sung out incessantly "down," "down!" as an admonition to those behind to dodge a projecting bough. The warning passed in an endless chorus along the column, but its very frequency defeated its kindness. For several hours we traveled in this manner, a squadron of involuntary hump-backs, every moment adding to the number of the hatless, bruised, and bloody. Then, beneath us were pitfalls, and mud-holes of unknown depth, and corduroys tumbled and broken, with many of the timbers sticking upright in the mud.

Travel over such ground was difficult and dangerous, speed impossible. It was far past midnight when we got clear of the woods, and halted at a plantation a mile or two beyond.

The place was deserted, except by a few negroes, who came out shyly, rubbing their eyes and doubting whether we were rebels or Yankees. Throwing out videttes, the command dismounted in the road, and built fires. Some warmed themselves with a hasty cup of coffee, and discussed the mishaps of the night, and the chances of a fight in the morning; while others, with their feet to the fires, slept the time away. The country about us seemed indescribably desolate: rugged and wooded and wild, with habitations few and far between. It had felt the tread of hostile armies only a few months previous, when the great Don Carlos was so handsomely, and perhaps willingly—

" Led by the nose, as asses are."

After resting for some time, we quietly moved on again. The morning was piercingly cold. Day-break found us still winding along in close column. The sun was delightful to our bodies, chilled by the frost of night, and to our eyes, weary of the monotonous gloom of forest, stream and road.

About a mile from Glasgow the advanced guard was reinforced and flankers thrown out—for it was not doubted that the wily John was but a little way before us.

Every ear was alert to catch the crack of carbines. But none came. The advance had now reached the top of a hill, at the base of which lay the town, and halted to reconnoitre. Developing nothing, our major, supposing that Morgan had drawn in his outposts and was awaiting us in the town, again reinforced the advance and ordered it to charge. Carbines were dropped, and sabres drawn—reins were tightly clutched—every man gathered his breath—for this was our maiden charge!

At the word, down the sloping road we trotted—a motley troop of bruised and clouted cavaliers—breaking soon into a gallop, and clattering with wild shouts into the square of the town.

The women and children, and old men, hurried to their doors—but still no shots! Parties were dispatched all over the place, but no armed foe appeared.

The major now arrived with the main column, and condescended to ask the Glasgowans, where was Morgan? "He'd been thar a yar ago," they said: "didn't know anything 'bout him now."

To say that we were chagrined and crest-fallen to have our rough ride and valiant charge turn out so tamely, would be saying only the truth. Some of the knowing ones declared that the whole adventure was a scheme to discipline our greenness, and get us into trim for real work further South.

But this theory was soon unsettled; for upon looking about the place, we discovered that Morgan's, or some other mounted force, had been there only a short time previous, as evidenced by many fresh horse-tracks and remnants of feed for man and beast, dispersed about in a method peculiar to cavalry.

With this crumb of comfort—the probable flight of Morgan at our approach—we turned our faces toward the southwest again. It was a cold and weary ride back over the country, by a different but no less difficult or desolate route, at one time getting lost and groping about for hours in the woods. Night had again settled around us ere the welcome hail of the picket ushered us once more to the comforts of camp.

IV.

DOWN INTO TENNESSEE.

A WEEK of rest and quiet at Bowling Green, and then we packed up for another long, but withal a pleasant ride, down into Tennessee. Our route was far more interesting and exciting than the march from Louisville. The country became more desolate as we advanced, and showed more recent marks of the presence of armies. Besides, Morgan was still skulking about, and we hoped that he might run against us accidentally—which did not happen, however.

Then, too, we had the mountains to cross. The southern portion of Kentucky is traversed by a spur of the Cumberland range, over which the highway leads into Tennessee. It was laborious work to transport the trains over these mountain roads. The way frequently leads along narrow ledges of rock, while chasms of unknown depth gape hideously around. Any restiveness or insubordination in a team might have plunged wagon and all over the precipice. At such places it was the custom to dismount the train-guards and string them out along the brink to keep the mules from approaching too near. Then there were gulleys and ravines to jolt through, and steep declivities to scale, requiring stout shoulders at the wheels.

But we crossed in one day without accident, and bivouaced for the night in a beautiful blue-grass field, under the shadow of the mountain. At noon of the next day we passed a perpendicular shaft of gray stone, about the size of a horse post, standing in the centre of the road, and—entered Tennessee.

There was something romantic in touching the soil of the old State. From our boyhood days the name had been embalmed in the songs of slavery and the stories of the border. To our imagination it was still in transition from the barbarous to the civilized—partly the haunt of the savage and the pioneer, as well as the home of the planter and his gang of happy slaves. One voice among us struck up the dirge of the poor old slave that went to rest 'way down in Tennessee; the sentiment was infectious, and in a moment more nearly the whole column was joining in the strain. The chorus gathered in volume, and rolled back in prolonged echoes from the mountains behind us, producing a remarkable, if not musical, effect. It seemed like the requiem of Slavery, then within a few days of dissolution.

The appearance of the country was now visibly changed. Beautiful, rolling land stretched away on every side, so unlike the rough hills and dead levels of Kentucky. But it was mournfully desolate. Houses along the road were, for the most part, deserted; and where they were not, only a few women and children appeared, staring in wondering silence at the passing Yankees. One village through which we passed was entirely uninhabited; houses and stores were open but empty; not a living thing was seen in the place. The fences along the road were stripped away, leaving only scattered heaps of black ashes and charred rails, around which had gathered in turn the Federals and Confederates.

On the evening of December 23 we arrived, tired with a day's brisk riding, at Tyree Springs in Sumner County, about twenty miles from Nashville. It was a lovely place, and before the war had been a favorite resort of the wealth and beauty of the south. The hotel was an immense structure, of wood, light and graceful, with verandahs from the foundation to the roof. Around the building clustered a beautiful wood, and down in a romantic hollow bubbled the Springs. Passing the place at sunset, there was no person visible, no doors or windows open, no sign or sound of life in the neighborhood. The unnatural loneliness of the spot was impressive and ominous.

We went into camp about half a mile further south, at the base of a slope that hid the buildings from view. Just after dark, in the midst of our horse-feeding and coffee-boiling, a bright reflection was observed over the trees in the direction of the Springs. The light rapidly increased in intensity and compass until the whole northern sky was illuminated. Soon the huge columns of smoke that began to roll up above the woods,

"With gloomy splendor red,"

confirmed too truly our fears that the hotel was on fire. From our picket-post at the top of the hill a sublime and terrible sight was presented. The immense building was wrapped in great sheets of flame, which forked wildly out from the windows and curled above the roof. It burned up with frightful rapidity. In less than an hour from the beginning the whole burning mass collapsed with a crash that shook the woods around, and sent great volumes of flame and smoke far up into the heavens.

The immensity of the structure, its elevated position, the gloomy and oppressive silence of the surroundings, and—more than all—the mysterious origin of the fire, combined to make a startling picture of war.

The Southern papers complained with just bitterness of the destruction of this place, but attributed it, of course, to Yankee vandalism. All I can say is that we had no hand in it, and that if our search of the neighborhood had succeeded in unearthing the incendiary, there would have been meted out to him a summary punishment.

Another day's slow march ensued, winding through bodies of infantry, interminable wagon-trains, and other evidences of proximity to the army.

At four o'clock we discerned through the dusty air the high walls and chimneys of the Rock City—and over all the dome of the Capitol—looming up grandly in the sunlight on the bluffs of the Cumberland. Passing through the pleasant suburb of Edgefield, we halted on the steep river-bank, to await the passage of a wagon-train over the pontoons. Before us were the remains of the suspension bridge destroyed by Bragg after the fall of Donelson. The wires still dangled from the abutments, and dipped into the river—a melancholy sight. Further down was the rail-road bridge, which had also been partly destroyed by Bragg, but was now repaired and in use by the Government.

We sat our horses impatiently until the stars came out; then, at six o'clock on Christmas eve, following the last wagon over the boat bridge, we scaled the steep south-bank and entered the city.

Inspiriting change! The streets were quiet and yet there was enough bustle and light and life, to make it seem like home to us, who had been a month in the wilderness. The very horses seemed to breathe new spirit as their hoofs touched the novelty of a paved street. We halted a few moments, during which the cake shops in the vicinity were hurriedly bought out by the hard-tacked troopers, to whom a gingerbread, howsoever musty and stale, was a luxury far above the steepest price that could be put upon it.

But we moved on again, clattering through the long treets, out into the southern suburbs, the lights and stir of the city sinking away into the gloom behind us. Turning off to the right at the end of College Street, we bivouaced on a slight eminence, grassy and wooded.

All around us was the buz of camps, and the horizon was aglow with a circle of innumerable fires, about which were gathered the fifty thousand soldiers of Rosecrans whom he had ordered to move on the 26th. The soldiers were celebrating the morrow with illuminations and amusements; and were jubilant, too, over the prospect of closing again with their old enemy on familiar ground— a new-born confidence, developed already by the genius of their new leader.

Our coming was hailed with congratulations from the neighboring regiments upon having arrived "just in time for the fight."

V.

THE STONE RIVER HOLIDAYS.

I SHALL never forget the melancholy sweetness of the *reveille* as sounded by bugler Murdoch on that morning after Christmas, eighteen hundred and sixty-two. Christmas-day, raw, damp, and disagreeable, had been depressing to the spirits, and the order to move, coming just after our five days' ride from Kentucky, had put us in no very good humor; added to which was a defection in our camp, six hundred men refusing to march: why and where fore, I purpose not to say here.

Upon the whole, it was a melancholy regiment; and when the strains of Murdoch's bugle, touched with an eloquence which only he could give, floated over the camp, they were in sad unison with, and helped to deepen, the general gloom. Ere the notes had died away I pulled aside the flap of my tent, and looked out. The sky was dark and solemn, the camp still silent. But one person was visible—Major Rosengarten, full-dressed, standing before his tent. He looked pale and handsome, and seemed to be listening to the last echoes of the *reveille*. Was it the voice of Fate, speaking to him in those dying notes, that paled his cheek and fixed his eye so vacantly?

The morning was damp and cheerless. Rain set in early —a hard, cold rain, which continued throughout that day and the next. The troops that had encircled us were already miles on the march. Nothing remained but the forlorn and dripping *debris* of the camps, and an occasional straggler searching in the ruins for plunder. We were the only regiment left to follow; and those of us who desired to go—say three hundred men—assembled by 8½ o'clock under the command of Majors Rosengarten and Ward.

An hour's trot on the Nolensville pike brought us up to the rear divisions of McCook, plodding merrily along in the rain and mud, joking betimes, and filing aside to allow our cavalcade to pass—not without remark, of course, for your "dough-boy" seldom looses an opportunity to gibe at his mounted comrade. Said one tired fellow, as he splashed along:

"Here comes these jockey-soldiers, ridin' over us; soft thing they have of it"

His remark was greeted with many approving comments.

"Bah!" growled an old sergeant, who had evidently seen both arms of the service, "it's not so soft as it seems, Charley. A fellow's got enough to do to take care of himself in a campaign like this, without havin' a horse to look to. Besides, when the fightin's over there's no rest for the trooper; he's got to go it always. Tell ye boys," continued the veteran, elevating his voice, " let them be cavalry that wants to be, I'd rather march this way and fight this way."

This reassured the discontented ones, for the man was evidently the oracle of his company.

A little further on we overtook the artillery, Edgarton's and Goodspeed's Ohio batteries—splendid organizations, already famed for their services under the lamented Mitchell. Edgarton was chief of artillery for Johnson's division, and rode proudly at the head of his guns, little dreaming that a few days hence would find them in the hands of Hardee, while he and his men would be hurried to a prison-pen in the heart of Dixie.

Thus on hour after hour. The rain continued to fall, the mud to deepen. There were frequent halts to await the clearing away of rebel skirmishers, and other obstructions. Far away to the left we could hear occasionly the faint patter of musketry, and the booming of heavier weapons, proving that Crittenden's men were at work.

The day waned rapidly under the leaden sky. At nightfall the rain respited us for an hour or so, and we turned off into a soaked field to bivouac, but had scarcely dismounted when the bugle again sounded to horse. Then out on the pike again, groping through the mud and darkness for several miles, until a house or two loomed up before us, and lights flickered through the windows.

It was Nolensville.

A short halt at the head-quarters of General Johnson resulted in moving us to a wet clover field near by. Therein stood two huge hay-stacks, which in five minutes were not so huge by a good deal. Our horses were unbridled, and gorged themselves on hay; while their masters, swallowing rain-soaked "tack," and lying crowdedly around the few small fires that were allowed, rested tolerably, notwithstanding an occasional sharp shower during the night.

At three o'clock on Saturday morning, the 27th December, we were aroused quietly by the orderlies. The morning was uncomfortably sharp, and a thick fog covered everything. Bridling up, we gathered silently around the smouldering embers of the fires. There was in every man an instinctive consciousness of being near " the front," that mysterious and eventful region so often referred to in the prints, and in the rear camps. There was no room to doubt it now. Evidently we had reached McCook's advance, and were about to lead it. The front! the rebels! under fire! These experiences, so long heard and read of and hoped for, were now at last to try our maiden courage.

What rousing letters we would write home, descriptive of charge, of hair-breadth 'scape, of victory !

But alas! who should survive to write them? Who now living of that martial group that gazed so abstractedly into the cinders, but will recall the manly figures and brave faces of those who never wrote *their* share of the campaign that followed ?

As soon as it was light enough to see a little way into the fog, we rode through the town and out the pike toward Triune, halting at a little log-house that stood on elevated ground, and commanded a view of some bold hills beyond. While we were peering through the mist, endeavoring to *see* something of the " front," there emerged from the log-house a portly, pleasant-faced General officer—R. W. Johnson, whose division occupied Nolensville. The General stood awhile talking with Major Rosengarten ; and from his gestures, and an occasional word caught, we now became satisfied that those hills, barely discernible through the fog, were held by the enemy's out-posts, and that there our first fight was to be.

So it proved. Our little command was divided into two equal squadrons, one to advance directly along the pike to Triune, the other to dislodge and push the rebels from the hills that skirted eastward from the road. This latter duty fell to Major Ward's party, which I follow.

Starting in advance of the other squadron, we moved down the road at a brisk trot. At the same time the fog lifted considerably, giving us a clearer view of the field. A short distance out we passed the infantry pickets, who hailed us with with such words as " go for 'em boys!" "give 'em thunder!" etc. (I say *thunder*, but that was not the precise word used.)

Reaching a favorable point, the Major ordered the fence on the left of the road to be taken down, which was done in a twinkling. Our party then filed over into a meadow, soft and miry, difficult to traverse—so much so that several horses were unable to keep up. We floundered through as fast as possible, skirted a cornfield, swept up a hill through a belt of timber, and descended into a wooded hollow, right under the enemy's position on the ridge. The column had not all entered the hollow, when *bang—bang, zip—zip,* came the rebel greeting. There was an immediate and general scattering to seek the protection of trees. We listened to the bullets until the novelty of their sound wore away, and then some attempt was made under our cover to return the enemy's fire; but the most careful scrutiny of the wooded heights above us failed to discover a foe.

"By George, Barney," whispered my mess-mate, Watts, "I see a gray back now; look! up there behind that short oak—he's stooping down. D—n him! I'll fetch him" —and while I watched the object, Watts carefully poised his carbine, and fired. The rebel did not move. I also fired; the smoke cleared away, but there still stooped the supposed gray-back.

"Thunder!" exclaimed my comrade, in disgust, "its only a stump."

And so we kept pegging away at stumps, under the impression that it was the soldier's duty to burn as many cartridges as possible. But the rebel bullets still came cutting through the tree tops, dropping the twigs and leaves.

The sound had become familiar, and as none of us had yet been hurt, we were slow to appreciate the danger of our situation. Now, however, a new peril appeared. Our virgin ears were startled by the roar of a field-piece from the unseen heights before us, and with a horrible *whir—r—r,* a rifled shot came plunging through the trees, and buried itself directly in front of my horse. Little "Shiloh" jumped back and trembled, as well he might. Hastily forming a line along the northern slope of the hollow, it was our Major's intention to charge up the declivity; but the line was not fairly completed before another deadly missile came crashing toward us, and, but for a stout tree that stopped its career, would have made sad havoc in our ranks. At the same time a trooper who had been sent forward to reconnoitre returned and reported that a charge would be impossible. It was plain that we must go at them by some other way.

Withdrawing from the hollow in good order, we struck a bee line, eastward, across the fields, to a point near the house of a Mr. Copeland, where the ridge before us was much less difficult of ascent. Here we formed a double line of battle, with skirmishers, and in that manner advanced resolutely over the hills, encountering no enemy.

They had withdrawn, hastened by the gallant charge of Rosengarten's squadron on the turnpike, the firing of which we had heard. Evidences of recent rebel presence met us at every step. Raw pork and meal, soaked in the rain; scattered corn, and embers emitting their last feeble smoke —these remains of the enemy were highly interesting to us green troops. One sanguine youth dismounted and secured an old bayonet scabbard, which he no doubt still preserves as a relic of his first battle field.

The rain now began to fall again. It would be hard to depict the extreme discomforts of that march. Hour after hour the rain fell heavily, with brief pauses, which were filled by a cold, cutting wind. Still we toiled on through the sodden fields, halting occasionly to reform our line when the nature of the ground broke it up.

We stopped at a large plantation house, fronting on a swollen creek. One of the horses had given out, and the rider must find another, or be left in the rear. I was ordered back with him to find a remount; so, loading the extra accoutrements on Shiloh, we started. It was an unwelcome task to toil back over those miry fields, knowing that the same ground must be traversed a third time in rejoining the command.

In an hour or so we reached Copeland's house, but (as we had expected) found his barn empty. An old negro man, the sole occupant of the premises, informed us that the master had sold his stock to the Confederates, and had gone off with them himself. The honest old fellow softened our disappointment admirably by filling our canteens with a capital article of applejack, and our haversacks with corn bread.

The horseless trooper, full of an energy imbibed from his canteen, shouldered his equipments, saddle and all, and set out for Nolensville, two miles distant; while I, shaking the generous black hand of our friend, turned my face once more to the front. Before riding away I took occasion to tell the negro that in a few days, on the first of the year, he would be a free man, and explained to him briefly the proclamation of President Lincoln. The innocent old soul regarded me all the while with a look of amused incredulity. He thought, no doubt, that under the influence of applejack I was endeavoring to perpetrate a grave joke upon him. Subsequently I learned with satisfaction that this man had fully realized the truth of my statements by becoming a soldier in the service of the United States.

Shiloh labored gallantly through the tough fields and driving rain, to the brick house where I had left the column. But the latter had gone. I followed the tracks over the creek for a mile, until they led me into a cedar-wood, where all trace disappeared. I was lost!

It was now near night-fall, rendered earlier by the clouded heavens. The prospect was uncomfortable. Should I plunge blindly forward, or await daylight there? In either case it was possible to fall into the enemy's hands.

The instinct of a brute is often sharper than human wit. The thought flashed upon me, and I resolved to trust to the dumb sagacity of my little horse. Loosing his rein, I gave him the spur, expecting that he would start off into the woods. Imagine my consternation when he stretched out his neck to nose the way, and turned abruptly to the rear again, out of the cedars! My faith in animal instinct wavered. I was about to turn him back again, having no idea of retreating, when he suddenly changed his course in another direction.

Two hours after I learned to my admiration that the command had actually entered the cedar woods and turned out again, taking the precise route followed by my horse.

It was a long, dark, and toilsome tramp. More than once I dismounted to ease the animal, intending to keep him company on foot; but the faithful beast would not stir unless I remained on his back.

Thus on, long after dark. How well I remember, when at length I emerged upon a hard road, and saw the welcome glimmer of camp fires in the distance! Riding up along a wooded ridge, I was brought to a stand by the hail of a picket. He passed me safely, but, I thought, reluctantly, as I was unable to give him the "chaw of tobacker" which he requested.

In a low field, immediately on the right, a few fires were glimmering, and figures of men and horses moved darkly about. Familiar voices came out of the gloom, and I knew that my comrades were there. Watts greeted me with a hurrah and a cup of coffee. Shiloh was unsaddled and made as comfortable as possible. The rain had mercifully ceased, but a slight snow had fallen—a most unpleasant night. Sleep, "sore labor's bath," came generously to our weary bodies; and when the bugle aroused us once more, we found the sabbath breaking clearly overhead, and the long-imprisoned stars, having peeped out before the dawn, were fainting away at the sun's approach.

There was a sharp rattle of musketry just ahead, the morning greeting of the pickets, but it soon died away.

What a quiet, beautiful Sunday it was, after the previous two days of gloom! We were in the vicinity of Triune, whence Hardee had retreated the previous evening. The brigade of infantry across the road from us packed up early and were off somewhere before we had saddled. There appeared to be no hurry for us. We made coffee and toasted pork at our leisure. The sun was two hours high before we mounted and moved slowly down the road. Even then there was no purpose apparent in our march. It began to be whispered about that the army would rest that day, and the knowing ones assured us that "Old Rosey" was a strict observer of the Sabbath, and would not willingly desecrate it by the shedding of blood.

A little way south of the town we dismounted in a grove, and stretched ourselves out upon the strewn leaves. How quiet was everything and everybody! The genial noon-day sun was rapidly warming the tired troopers into slumber, when lo! a courier from head-quarters, with the regimental mail.

It was our first since leaving Bowling Green, and for awhile there was a lively scene. The son, the brother, the lover, the husband, there on the eve of battle, greedily devoured the dear messages from those who, with anxious and tearful hearts, would await reply—many, alas, still waiting! Groups were gathered about the few who had received newspapers—the *Press* and *Tribune* a fortnight old—telling how Burnside had failed at Fredericksburg. A few isolated themselves to write up their diaries, or to pencil hasty replies to letters.

"MOUNT!"

The command came, swift and sudden, without warning. Letters and papers were hastily crammed away. The woods echoed with the jingle of sabres and the stirring of leaves as we mounted and trotted off down the road, across a deep creek—the bridge over which had been destroyed by the rebels the night before—altogether a distance of three miles, halting at the house of a Mr. Pett. It was a pleasant place, surrounded by orchards and corn-fields. We were on the road to Eagleville, by which Hardee had retreated, and it was suspected that his scouts were in the neighborhood, making Pett's house their head-quarters. On the porch stood two young ladies, with whom our Majors talked politely. But the girls were spirited Confederates, and did not appreciate Yankee civility. One of them displayed a pocket pistol, with which she threatened to blow out the brains of one of our officers who had presumed to address her. The premises were searched, but the girls were apparently the only occupants.

. After listening awhile to their unwomanly bluster we returned to the creek. Toward sunset, however, another alarm was given, and we again dashed forward to the place. This time the house and surroundings underwent a thorough scrutiny, the ladies all the while threatening terrible vengeance.

"Mark my words," exclaimed she of the pistol, "you cowardly Yankees will go flying back to Nashville to-morrow quicker than you came — though I hope to Heaven"—here she raised her clenched fist—"that not one of you will live to reach there."

The lady was not naturally pretty, but the dramatic excitement of the speech gave color to her cheek and fire to her eye; while her earnest boldness commanded our respect. Not a few brutes among us, however, allowed their low instincts to triumph in derisive laughter. Her wish, alas! was partly fulfilled, as will duly appear.

Finding no secreted enemies in the house, we at sunset fell back again to the creek, and prepared to picket it for the night. A line of posts was established, extending from the junction of two roads on our left, to the Triune pike on our right, a distance of over a mile. The party with which I was detailed took post at the ford, near the remains of the bridge, our videttes being doubled and thrown across the ford a score of yards toward Pett's, commanding a view of the road as far as his house.

The night was frosty and moonlight. Watts and I went out on post for the last time at 4 o'clock on Monday morning—just the time, from that to daylight, when attacks on outposts are usually made. As we were holding the extreme right of the army, it was probable that the enemy's cavalry would be on the alert to develope our position. We were therefore instructed to be very vigilant.

The first hour passed away in silence—the next was the most dangerous. Our eyes were kept fixed upon the road by Pett's house, for at that point we expected every minute to see the foe start up darkly against the horizon.

Suddenly our attention was drawn to a rustling among the corn-stalks, away over in the field on our right. It ceased for a little while, but was soon detected again.

"Do you hear that, Barney?" whispered my companion.

"I do—we must look sharp."

The silence for the next interval—the strain upon our eyes and ears—was excruciating. Again we heard the noise, more subdued but evidently nearer than before. Acting upon the same instinct, we both quietly and quickly dismounted, and posted ourselves at the fence that skirted the corn-field. Kneeling there, and holding our bridles with the left arm, we rested carbines on the middle rail of the fence, and awaited the enemy. We had no doubt at all that a rebel had left his hiding place at Pett's, and was approaching us in this stealthy way to pick us off.

After another fearful silence, the sound came again, startlingly distinct and near, accompanied by the cautious *tread of feet.* On came the miscreant, stopping every instant or two, as if to listen and peer ahead. Not more than six yards now intervened between us and the foe ; but we could see nothing in the tall, close corn.

The suspense of that moment was painful and profound —I recall it now with a thrill, and so, no doubt, will my companion. Not that we were more nervous than soldiers usually are; but one may calmly face an open foe, and yet shudder at the creep of an assassin.

The next instant we should have fired blindly into the corn, when directly before us the stalks were thrust aside and there appeared in the waning light of the moon—reader, what do you suppose? Why, only the big ears and head of a white jackass! *There* was our assassin, assinine and innocent, munching the fodder at his ease, unconscious of the terror which he had inspired, and of the tragic death which he had narrowly escaped. Immensely relieved, we arose before the beast as suddenly as apparitions, and he he in turn was frightened into a hasty retreat.

The joke leaked out—it was too good to keep to ourselves —and to this day Watts and I are known to many of the boys as the pickets who were bushwhacked by an ass.

Monday dawned clear and cold. At eight o'clock no enemy had appeared. We were relieved by infantry, and the command fell back to Triune, where we found our wagons, and replenished haversacks for two days more.

Major Rosengarten, then, under orders, detailed thirty men to act as train guard, and with the rest of the three hundred started off on the southern flank of McCook,

5

who was now moving eastward to concentrate with the centre and left.

The wagon guard consisted of the newly relieved pickets, so that Watts and I were included—not greatly to our regret. Being directed to await orders at Triune, and anticipating some hours of quiet, we prepared to provide for the inner man such luxuries as the neighborhood afforded. Some successful foraging was done. The whole party dined regally on fresh mutton and pork, goose, chicken, etc., with enough left for another day. Government meat was at a heavy discount. With full bellies and jovial spirits we lounged in groups about the fires, recounting the incidents of the previous few days, and voting unanimously that campaigning was not so terrible after all, when opportunity like the present offered compensation. Some of the boys had secured a quantity of applejack from a neighboring still. Canteens were freely circulated and pipes went round. Conversation grew genial and mirthful. The pickets who had been bushwhacked the night before came in for raillery. Songs were sung— "Gay and Happy," and others of that ilk—with a vehemence that argued well for the strength of the applejack. Ah yes, the boys were happy, very happy; and noisy——

So noisy that we did not hear the thunder of hoofs on the road until a horseman was almost in our midst. He was a courier from our command. With pale face and excited utterance he told this fearful story: that the regiment had been ambuscaded by a heavy force of rebel infantry, and that the two Majors, four Sergeants, and several privates, were known to be dead; others wounded and missing.*

---

*In this charge there were eleven killed, twenty-five wounded, and nine missing.

There was no more song or mirth that day. The tidings seemed incredible, but confirmation and detail were swift to follow, and the horrors of the story were more than verified. They had discovered what they supposed to be a small force of rebels secreted behind a brush-fence; charging across the fields to within a few yards of the enemy, they were met by a long sheet of flame from two regiments of infantry, with the result above stated,—except that Major Ward was not instantly killed, but lingered a little while at a house near the scene of the slaughter.

With this terrible news came orders to move the train on the morrow across the country to the Murfreesboro turn-pike, and rejoin the command near the headquarters of General Rosecrans.

It was a melancholy night, that. Around the fires, in low, sad voices, the calamity was discussed, and the mysterious presentiments of some of the killed were made known. Herring had written a line to his wife, on the fly-leaf of his pocket bible, to the effect that he was about to be killed. Kimber had, that morning, been unusually anxious to wash his face, and upon being asked in a jocular way why he was so particular, replied, with a sad smile, that he would "make a better looking corpse." Rosengarten had at starting expressed the belief that he would not come back alive. Ward had a noticeable depression of spirits, which even his natural gaiety could not conceal. .

Both the Majors were young, well-connected, ambitious and daring; and though perfectly friendly to each other, there was an ill-concealed rivalry between them which sought comparison in personal gallantry. They were supposed to be constantly in search of enterprises that promised a field for such display.

They had found one, the first and the last. Their rivalry was ended, and equal glory was their meed.

The "wee sma' hours" were upon us ere the gloom created by the day's tragedy was forgotten in slumber. Even there it followed *me*. In a dream I again opened the flap of my tent, and saw the melancholy figure standing alone, listening to the voice of that fate which had now closed about him forever.

The life of a soldier in the field gives him little room for sentiment. The scenes crowd each other; the excitements of each day are forgotten in those next following. So that when the morning of Tuesday, December 30, dawned upon us, and we bustled about for breakfast, and packed up to march, there was a visible return of philosophy and good cheer.

All that morning we jogged along with our five wagons, through a wild, wooded country, impeded in our march by the roughness of the roads. At noon we had made but half a dozen miles. We halted, then, at a sharp turn in the road, and near by stood a cabin from which the smoke curled up into the air, showing it to be inhabited. Several of our fellows, having consumed their mutton, and still holding the Commissary in contempt, rode up to the house with the hope of buying something eatable. Watts and myself brought forth the remnants of a boiled goose. Sitting our horses thus comfortably, in the warm sunshine of noon, we listened anon to the faint sound of skirmishing that came up from the south, and congratulated ourselves on being in the rear and out of danger.

Suddenly we noticed two or three troopers scampering wildly from the house, and through the woods behind the latter caught sight of a party of rebel horsemen approaching the road. We had not time to recover from our astonishment—indeed, I was half-inclined to believe that the strangers were friends, as two of them wore blue over-coats—when they began to fire at us. Watts had his horse's ear slit by the first bullet. We were about getting our carbines into position, when an immense crowd of brown-coated cavalry appeared in the woods behind the first party, and swarmed toward us.

We did not wait to see any more. Our whole party, teamsters and all, commenced a masterly retreat in every direction, every man for himself. The rebels kept up a constant peppering at the fugitives, and shouted to them to surrender. Many of them complied, and were paroled (and robbed) on the spot, to find their way as best they could to Nashville. The victors then cut the mules loose, and set fire to the wagons.

All this while, as may be expected, Watts and I were getting out of the way. He had the fastest horse, so that his retreat in the matter of speed was more masterly than mine. But after a good, long, rough three miles of gallop, I overtook him, together with a small party of the Third Tennessee Cavalry. This regiment had been dispersed elsewhere by the same rebel force, now ascertained to be Wheeler's. That General was making his famous raid around the army of Rosecrans, and was fresh from his sore repulse at Lavergne.

The officer in command of the Tennesseeans got the stragglers together and would have followed the rebels, with the hope of saving a wagon or two; but more escaped men came by and reported the total destruction of the train.

My blanket fellow and myself held a counsel of war, and decided upon our course. We made our way as fast as possible through a wretched country, in the direction, as we supposed, of the Murfreesboro pike. About dark we emerged from the forest upon a turnpike. Following it up to and across Overall's Creek, we began to overtake the ambulances and wagons of Davis and Sheridan, and learned to our disgust that this was the Wilkerson road, two miles west of the one we were seeking. The troops of McCook had advanced along this pike during the day, fighting themselves into position. Evidences of conflict met us at every step—numerous dead bodies, wounded stragglers, scattered arms and accoutrements, trees shivered by shot and shell.

Tired out with the day's work, Watts and I were loth to go further that night, although anxious to rejoin our command. The latter was supposed to be somewhere on the Murfreesboro road, near the general head-quarters; but to find it then would have necessitated a night's blind traveling through a wilderness of cedars. We concluded to await daylight.

We were now at Grierson's farm, a mile south of Overall's creek. On elevated ground to the left of the road, opposite the orchard, were some ammunition wagons belonging to Sheridan's division. Making known our situation to the teamsters they welcomed us to their fires with soldierly hospitality, and put us in the way of procuring corn for our horses.

The night was clear and cold—so clear that I made some notes in my diary by the light of the moon. We were about three miles from Murfreesboro, not more than one mile from our own front. Our position gave us a view of the southern horizon, which was lighted up with the fires of the enemy. Rockets occasionally shot into the air. By attentive listening we could hear the rumbling of rail-road trains, and at times a confused murmuring like the cheers of a distant multitude. The fire-works and cheers were in honor of the Confederate President's visit to Bragg at Murfreesboro, as we learned next day from prisoners.

The hostile armies were now face to face. For five days they had been sparring—one pushing, the other receding; closing slowly together until the distance between them was reduced to less than usual skirmish ground. The struggle must come on the morrow.

How many gallant souls were sleeping then their last temporal sleep! dreaming perhaps of the homes they were never more to see!

How many homes and hearts far away would be swiftly and forever plunged into desolation by the first news from this battle-field!

With such thoughts—for "the weary way had made us melancholy"—I and my bunk-fellow bestowed ourselves into a wagon, on some boxes marked "Enfield Cal. 58," and there awaited the coming of the memorable last day of the year.

It was not yet daylight when the mules around us, having disturbed our slumber more than once during the night by their kicking and rattling of chains, roused us thoroughly by a concerted braying for breakfast. Our teamster friends were already astir. We got up, fed and saddled our horses, and breakfasted bountifully on a cracker and a half and a cup of coffee. By that time the streaky clouds in the east were receiving the first tints of the sun. The morning was intensely cold, and a heavy frost covered everything. Riding down the turnpike to a dirt road that branched westward past Grierson's house, Watts dismounted to tighten his saddle-girth. He had not completed the operation when we both were startled by a sharp, swift volley of musketry, that echoed from beyond the cedars away to the south-west. It must have been two minutes before another volley was heard, deeper and heavier, followed by the roar of artillery. Quickly another crash, and another roar, mingled with irregular reports; and then they followed each other rapidly, and seemed to be spreading more to our front.

"Watts," said I, as we started forward again, "that's more than a skirmish."

"Yes," said he, oracularly, pulling out his watch, "its the battle of Murfreesboro, begun at ten minutes past seven o'clock A.M. on the last day of the year, 1862."

On the strength of our faith in the prediction, we both pulled out our note books, and recorded it in the prophet's words.

Further on, at a clearing in the cedars, we stopped again and listened to the increasing tumult of the conflict. The rebel cheers, as they drove our men, were plainly audible. A couple of demoralized artillerymen came hurrying out of the woods from the direction of the battle, and in answer to our inquiries reported an overwhelming rout—brigades and regiments and bat'eries surprised and broken to pieces by the swiftness and vigor of the rebel attack.

But it was all important to ourselves that we should hurry on. Our purpose was to get as near as possible to our own lines, and follow them eastward to the Murfreesboro road. Proceeding briskly along the pike, the noise of the battle grew louder. Frequent stragglers came running from the thicket, some mounted on mules, some on artillery horses, cut from the wagons and guns.

The turn of affairs was evidently disheartening to the troops. Probably not one soldier in the army had anticipated such a thing as our own defeat after five days' successful advance.

Emerging from the cedar-woods upon an open country, the uproar of the conflict met us in full force. Half a mile distant, along the edge of another cedar thicket, stretched a line of blue coats extending to the left across the pike and into the woods beyond it. Here the fighting was stubborn, and while we remained, the enemy made no progress; but on the right the sound of the battle surged frightfully toward the rear, and the dull, white smoke was gathering heavily over the trees in that direction.

We observed, too, that the turnpike in our rear, as far as the eye could reach, was darkened with retreating troops. A confused mob of soldiers, most of them without arms, were hurrying across the road and plunging into the cedar-brakes. Great numbers, mostly wounded, were also falling back from the divisions in front of us. Slowly and wearily the bloody and bandaged heroes passed us by, some of them horribly mutilated, yet silent in their suffering, and still clinging to their muskets.

A little way before us, off the road, we noticed a mounted group, from which occasionally an aide or orderly dashed off to the front. Evidently some one in authority was there. Riding nearer we saw in the midst of the party a small, precise figure, well seated on a black horse. There was one star on his shoulder, and he was talking or giving orders in a brief and quiet way.

This was Sheridan—not so famous then, but well known and admired in the army. He was even then building the foundation of his fame. It was his division that was fighting so stoutly on the edge of the cedars, and won for him that day the additional star of a Major-General.

All this while the crash and roar of the battle shook the earth beneath us. The rattle of musketry sounded like the continuous ripping of heavy canvas: imagine that sound magnified a thousand times or so, and you have an idea of the noise of battle. The stragglers became more numerous. Bullets and shells were hurtling around and over us in a lively manner. The place was getting uncomfortable.

Watts and myself had no business there; we had stopped merely out of curiosity, anyhow—so we reasoned ourselves very conveniently into a retreat. Following the stragglers, our intention was to make all haste across the country; but passing so many wounded soldiers it occurred to us to put a couple of disabled boys astride of our horses. An hour's tedious meandering through the cedar wilderness brought us to the open country, bordering the Murfreesboro road. Along the latter, and far to the left of it, we observed dark masses of troops, moving to the aid of the retreating right. The country in the rear was crowded with disorganized regiments; and as the waves of battle continued to surge nearer from all points of the line, it became evident to the stupidest observer that the whole army was retrograding.

Reaching the Murfreesboro road, we transferred our wounded freight to an ambulance, and soon found our regiment, which was preparing to move.

It was about eleven o'clock when we were joined by the 7th Pennsylvania, and portions of the 3d Tennessee, and 2d Kentucky Cavalry. Twelve rounds of cartridge were distributed as we sat our horses. Then we rode off under the lead of Brig. Gen. D. S. Stanley, Chief of Cavalry.

It was a long and wild ride that he led us, over the country on the right flank of the retreating army, crossing and re-crossing Overall's Creek. Going head-long on the outskirts of a wood, the column was startled by the near roar of artillery behind us. A shell exploded in our midst, and it was soon discovered that a private of the 7th Pennsylvania had lost an arm. Another shot came. The column got restive, and the rear half made a plunge for safety along a narrow road that seemed inviting; but the fugitives ran straight into the arms of Wheeler's Rebel Cavalry. Among these captured troopers was my boon companion, Watts.

Meantime, the other portion of the brigade was getting demoralized—for the battery had fired a third shot—when we were presently reassured by the statement that the supposed rebel gun was our own, and had fired into us by mistake. Poor consolation, that, for the 7th Pennsylvania boy!

Pushing on through woods and by-roads we about four o'clock emerged upon a dirt-road near the house of a Mrs. Burrows. The first thing I noticed on coming into the road was the dead body of a mere boy, not more than fifteen years old, lying with his face half buried in a pool of mud. His arms were outstretched, and his right hand grasped the barrel of an old rifle that lay beside him. In passing the body I noted with a shudder that some of the horses had trampled on the skull. Over a fence, just behind the boy, lay an old man, he also clinging to his rifle. Both were clad in the merest rags, and the old man's hat still partly covered his head. They had evidently fallen at the same time—the boy just after clearing the fence, the old man in the act of climbing.

Looking off down the field, numerous other bodies were seen, some in blue uniform. In an orchard, on the other side of the road, were half a dozen Union corpses, as evidenced by the absence of their overcoats and hats, and, in some instances, of their shoes. The poorly-clad Confederates could never resist the temptation to plunder a dead Yankee in that manner.

We took down the fence, near the old rebel's body, and filed over into the field. It was beautiful ground, covered with short grass, and sloped away gently for half a mile, rising into a bold ridge at the southern extremity.

Half way down the slope we formed a line of battle. I looked back over our rear and distinguished a dark-blue streak, stretching along the edge of some timber, about

half a mile distant. I could see, too, the faint flash of a
bayonet now and then. We were supported by infantry,
it seemed—a most comforting thought.

General Stanley and staff rode slowly up and down before us, scanning carefully the ridge in the south. From
that point, evidently, the rebels were expected. The sun
was low in the west, when faint and confused firing was
heard from the front, followed by the rapid and disorderly
flight of our skirmishers, back over the ridge, and from
the woods that covered the right of our line. Almost immediately after, a few mounted figures appeared and halted
on the ridge—it was the enemy. More followed; then a
long column filed up over the hill, and down the slope a
short distance, where they wheeled very prettily into line.
A second column soon followed and performed the same
manœuvre. Their skirmishers advanced boldly to the
base of the hill, and commenced firing at ours. There
was artillery, too, we noticed, posted in a clump of trees
on the rebel left.

Meanwhile there was agitation along our lines. General Stanley came thundering down from the left, and
stopped short before the commanding officer of the 7th
Pennsylvania.

"Major," he said, "we'll charge them now." He then
dashed past us to the Tennesseeans on our right, where he
spoke similar words of cheer. Returning to the centre, he
said, in a voice that rang like a trumpet,

" *I* will take command of the 15th Pennsylvania."*

---

* It was a graceful and fatherly kindness in General Stanley to take
personal command of our little battalion, for we were almost orphaned
of officers. The Colonel had been a prisoner at Richmond since the
battle of Antietam; the Lieut.-Colonel was an invalid at Nashville,
whence he started with us, but was compelled to return; the two
Majors, whom we had learned to confide in and admire, were dead.
Captain Vezin, to whom the command had suddenly succeeded, though
a brave and worthy officer, was comparatively untried and unknown.

With that he drew his sword, shouted the command, *"Draw Sabre! Charge! Follow me!"* and plunged away down the slope with his little brigade at his heels.

It was gallantly done. The red sunset glanced like blood upon our twelve hundred blades as we swept like an avalanche upon the foe.

The rebels opened upon us with artillery, and stood their ground until we had come to close quarters with their skirmishers. Then their first line gave way, bearing back the second, the whole mass scampering off in confusion up the ridge. Their guns were hastily limbered and drawn off. In fifteen minutes from the start, not an armed foe was in sight. A dozen or so were killed, and over a hundred captured. Our casualties amounted to a few wounded.

One of the men of my company (L),* performed an act of brilliant daring. As the rebels were hurrying away he dashed forward into a crowd of them, shot down the color-bearer of a regiment, snatched the flag from his grasp as he fell, and bore it triumphantly but modestly to his comrades. This action was performed under the eye of General Stanley, who complimented the hero on the field.

Alas! hero though he was—like many another of that day—he did not long enjoy his laurels. Two weeks thereafter he died of disease in a hospital at Nashville.

The memorable day was ended, but not our danger and suffering. All night long we sat on horseback in that field, expecting an attack at daylight. The cold was most bitter. We had eaten nothing since morning; both men and horses were nearly used up. Still we were kept there, snatching such sleep as we could on horseback, and agitating our hands and feet to keep them from freezing.

---

* Hoyt.

When the dawn came, raw and misty, the first of the New Year, it found us crusted with frost, benumbed and shivering, looking wearily through leaden eyelids for the expected enemy. But the rebels were probably as fagged as we, for they did not appear.

At sunrise, relieved by infantry, we fell back over the fields to the pike again, passing scores of corpses, frozen stiff and covered with a winding-sheet of frost. Over one of these bodies some friendly hand had thrown a blanket, to which a scrap of paper was fastened, bearing no doubt the data for a rude memorial when the burial-party should come.

My story of these eventful holidays ends here. For though that New Year's day was not without adventure —among others a rebel attack upon a train which we were escorting to Nashville—yet our participation in the great battle ended with the dawn of the New Year.

VI.

THE COURIER LINE.

OF all the duties performed by our soldiers in this war, none were more dangerous or exciting than those of the courier. True, the infantry and artillery fought the pitched battles, and the cavalry led the advance, held the outposts, or made long rides around the enemy's flanks; but they were conducted in person by officers of judgment and experience, and, besides, individual danger is immeasurably lessened by facing it *en masse.*

To the courier, however, were intrusted the written commands for the movements of the army, with which he was expected to make his way *alone* (unless particular danger was foreseen) through a country that was probably penetrated by the enemy's scouts or infested by the more dreaded guerrillas.

We had just got settled into camp again, at Trenton, Georgia, after the laborious scaling of Sand Mountain, when, early one bright starry morning, the orderlies shook us out from the comfortable blankets, with injunctions to pack everything and saddle up immediately. Then away on a long and dusty, but withal a pleasant, starlight ride across the valley, passing the rear camps of McCook and Thomas, from which the *reveille* was beating merrily in the crisp morning air. These corps were on the march to cross the Lookout Mountains, which loomed up grandly in the distance. We were not long in discovering the nature of our new duties. As we proceeded, details of five or six men, under a non-commissioned officer, were left at convenient points along the road; these were stations or reliefs on the courier line which we were forming. Our station was the most remote from the head-quarters of the army, while the constant advance of the different corps left us every day more isolated. Still more trying was the fact that our route to the advancing columns lay over the gloomy and difficult passes of the Lookout range, to surmount which taxed the utmost efforts of man and beast. Those who have served only in the eastern armies can form but a slight idea of the extraordinary feats of strength and endurance performed by the western troops in scaling the mountains of Tennessee and Georgia. The theatre of the war in Virginia presents no such formidable barriers as were encountered and overcome by the armed woodmen of the west.

It was about ten o'clock on a cool night in the early part of September. Our little cabin blazed with a cheerful fire, which sent a gleam of dancing light out through the open doorway and across the road. The couriers, belted and spurred, stood or reclined in all sorts of positions around the fire, silently awaiting despatches. We had learned to be expectant at night, as experience had proved that the majority of the mysterious packages came through at that time. Sergeant D. had just made a remark to that effect, when the familiar sound of horse's feet broke upon our ears. Mine were, perhaps, more alive to the sound at that moment than the rest, it being my turn to carry the next despatch. I walked to the door to listen. By the speed of the approaching messenger, I knew that the missive he carried was in haste. In advance of his arrival, therefore, I proceeded to mount "Shiloh," who was in excellent trim, and rubbed his nose briskly on my shoulder as I untied him. He knew right well that a long and perilous journey was to be made, and like a brave animal as he was, his nostrils snorted defiance.

In another moment the courier arrived. Sergt. D, examined the despatch, and handed it to me as I rode up to the door. By the light from within I glanced at the superscription and read: "Major General Thomas, commanding 14th Corps. *Full speed.*" An instant later I was galloping away.

The night was very clear, but chilly. As the cool air penetrated my clothing, I found myself more than once turning in the saddle to catch a farewell glimpse of the bright doorway behind, and the cheerful track across the road. But those beacons of comfort faded gradually in the distance, and as I descended a gentle slope in the road they finally disappeared. I then braced myself anew for the weary ride. Four long miles to the mountains, four still longer miles to climb and descend those wild gaps; and Heaven only knew how much further after that, as the 14th Corps was probably still moving. I had traversed those roads several times before at night, but on this occasion they appeared to be unusually gloomy. The fenceless fields by which I swept seemed more forlorn than usual; the woods were darker through which I felt my way; the hideous cry of the owls seemed to fill the air with demon voices. I could not shake from me the presentiment of some impending evil. Instinctively my hand sought the revolver at my side, and half-cocked it. The action caused Shiloh to prick up his ears and increase his speed, and in a short time I found myself under the bold brow of Lookout, which shut out half the heavens, and rendered the darkness more intense. The approach to the mountain lies through a dense woods, along the outer skirt of which flowed a small stream, rippling musically in its narrow bed. Approach-

ing the creek, I loosened the rein in order to allow my
horse to drink, as he was accustomed to do at this place.
The banks were rather steep, and as he lowered his nose
and was about to feel his way into the water, the woods
behind were torn into a million echoes by the report of a
rifle! At the same time my horse plunged madly forward
into the creek, lost his footing, and we both went down
together. It will readily be believed that I was scared; but
I preserved sufficient presence of mind to disengage my
feet from the stirrups and to draw my pistol, which I held
up out of the water. The current of the stream was neither
deep nor strong, so that Shiloh and myself soon regained
our feet, and made all haste up the opposite bank. It was
not until that moment that I noticed a mounted figure
darkly outlined on the other side of the stream. It was
my would-be murderer, who had doubtless expected to find
me dead or disabled. I gave him a positive assurance to
the contrary by discharging a shot at him, which caused
the figure to disappear as suddenly as it had come. I
listened to the sound of the rascal's retreat until it died
away in the distance. Then, wringing some of the water
out of my clothes, and remounting, I pushed forward with
all speed from what appeared to be a dangerous locality.

But my horse had not proceeded twenty yards before I
perceived that his strength was failing. His steps lagged
more and more every moment, in spite of my utmost efforts
to urge him forward. With a heavy heart I dismounted
and examined him. My fears proved too true: he was
wounded. I felt a perforation in his groin, from which the
warm blood oozed slowly down his flanks. The brave
beast finally succumbed, and with a deep drawn sigh
staggered heavily to the ground. For awhile my own
danger was forgotten in sympathy for the poor horse. He
had borne me faithfully and well through a thousand perils,

and now he was giving up his life in my service. I am
not ashamed to confess that the expiring breath of Shiloh
as it ascended from those wild woods wrung from my eyes
a tear of anguish and regret, though long a stranger to the
"melting mood."

My situation was certainly alarming. The bushwhack-
er might follow me, and it was equally probable that others of his clan were lying in advance, to make sure of the
victim. Those dreadful marauders seldom traveled alone.

For aught I knew their practiced eyes might even then
be staring through the darkness around me. For a
moment or two I was in a painful state of indecision. In
night rides I had always trusted implicitly to the instinct of
my horse; but now that resource was denied me, and my
topographical instincts were none of the best. Should I
make my way back to the station, remount and bring a
comrade with me? Perish the thought! I said. A
feeling of pride determined me to go forward at all haz-
ards and deliver my despatch. Quickly stripping the
bridle, blanket, and saddle-bags from the dead animal,
and securing them about my person, I gave my belt an
extra hitch, bade a mental farewell to the carcass of Shiloh,
and started forward.

By the position of the few stars that were visible I
assumed the time to be near midnight. The road up the
mountain was fearfully trying to legs and wind. For two
hours (as I judged) I clambered up the rocky way, stopping
every hundred yards to rest my limbs and fill my exhausted lungs. The air grew colder as I neared the summit,
and the heavy dew saturated my cap and great-coat, already
well soaked in the creek. It was growing lighter, too, as
I ascended. I turned at times to look off into the valley
behind, which stretched away dark and shadowy to the
horizon. Almost beneath my feet, as it seemed, I caught

an occasional glimpse of a gleam of light, which twinkled in the distance like a star. It was the bright doorway I had left behind. How like home it seemed, then, in the rude walls of the courier's hut!

But like the "Excelsior" boy, I turned away with a sigh from the "household fires," and bent my steps again toward the summit. I had not gone far when "Halt! who comes there?" yelled out shrill and clear, as if from the clouds. The unexpected challenge thrilled me to the marrow. Was it a rebel or a Union picket? The lightning-like process by which I arrived at the conclusion that my challenger was a Federal sentry, is long since forgotten; but to such a conclusion I did arrive in an instant. Answering—

"A courier with despatches,"

"Dismount, courier, and advance," he replied.

As I was already dismounted—and would have been on those steeps, even if I had had my horse—I proceeded to obey the latter part of the injunction. I had gone but a few yards, however, when I was halted again. "Where's your horse"? inquired the sentinel, who was evidently growing suspicious. This question led to an explanation of affairs; and in a short time I was the centre of a gaping crowd on the mountain top, to whom I related my adventure in the valley. My listeners were a portion of Harrison's Mounted Infantry, who were returning from a scout. I hold in grateful remembrance a tin-cup full of hot coffee, which one of these brave boys prepared for my benefit. I think they called him "Gussy." Long may he wave! unless, poor fellow, he sleeps under the blood-soaked soil of Chickamauga, the omens of which conflict were then gathering at the front. ·Aided by the advice of these boys, and a captured mule which they loaned me, I was not long in finding the way into the other valley, where the newly risen sun and freshly traveled roads enabled me to keep track of the 14th Corps. I found the Head-Quarters of Pap Thomas in the saddle, and delivered my despatch to one of his staff.

VII.

CHICKAMAUGA—LOOKOUT MOUNTAIN.

IT was the night of September 19, 1863. The first day of the awful conflict on "Dead Man's River" had passed into history—a bloody page. The contending armies, mutually exhausted, sank down among the dead in those dark forests to snatch a few hours rest ere the sun should light them again to the murderous work of battle.

Our company had moved in the morning from Crawfish Springs with the head-quarters train, and since 3 P.M. had been standing to horse towards the extreme left, a little east of the Rossville road. Here we had snuffed the odor of the battle on our right, and listened impatiently to the crash and roar, the yell of the charge, and the cheer of the repulse. But we could see nothing of the troops, save a frequent straggler looking for, or skulking from, his regiment, and more frequently a wounded soldier seeking a surgeon. The ambulances, too, rolled by us constantly with their freight of human suffering. Towards evening Minty's splendid brigade of horsemen trotted past us in the direction of Rossville, to meet the enemy's cavalry in our rear. Only those who have experienced the feeling can know the misery of inactivity on the field of battle.

Now that night had fallen, and the fight died away—the result of it, too, being doubtful—we began to grow exceedingly restive. Our Lieutenant Commanding rode uneasily up and down in front of us. He evidently shared our anxiety. I think he would soon have taken the responsibility of moving somewhere, had we not heard the sound of rapid hoofs down the road. The command mounted in a twinkling, and awaited developments, which might be the firing of our videttes, or the welcome appearance of a courier. It *was* a courier, bringing orders for us to make all haste to Chattanooga.

We had now something active to do, and we did it. A wild and breathless ride ensued. The road was inches deep with dust, and it was rarely that a trooper could see the head of the horse that carried him. Occasionally, though, a little breeze wafted the dust clouds away, revealing a hazy moon, and along our left the low dark ridges of the Mission Hills, overshadowed by the lofty range of Lookout.

We overtook thousands of silent stragglers, many of them wounded; and picked our way through miles of wagons, falling back to the Tennessee. At John Ross's house—called "Rossville"—we found the reserve corps of Gordon Granger resting on their arms. We halted for a short time among the Ohio boys of General Steadman, who little dreamed that their timely march on the morrow would save the hard-pressed heroes on the Chickamauga. Moving on again, through dust thick enough to cut with our sabres, we reached Chattanooga about midnight. Utterly worn out—for we had been unusually active on the courier line, and for four days past had not unsaddled—men and beasts threw themselves on the ground at the rail-road depot and slept.

The dawn of Sunday, the 20th September, gave us our first view of the objective point of the campaign.

The first object that challenged attention was the magnificent dark blue front of Lookout Mountain, wreathed in the vapors that rose like incense from the river at its feet. The sun, though to us unrisen, tipped the bald pate of the mountain with a golden streak, while the ridges and valleys below yet lay in the mists of early dawn.

The town—itself a straggling, disordered place—was full of straggling soldiers. Wagon trains crowded through the town and rumbled over the pontoons to the north side of the Tennessee.

Meanwhile we breakfasted on the remnants of our rations issued three days previous, and drew quarter rations for two days more. The memorable starving time, which for the rest of the army, began with the siege, commenced for us on this Sunday morning. Not that provisions were scarce, but the Commissary Department had probably already received orders to hoard up their stores. For the horses we were compelled to cross the river and rummage some miles, through a well gleaned country, before we could find them a little fodder.

Returning to the river we bivouaced on the north bank in front of the town. Here we lay throughout that long, eventful Sunday, watching the arrival of the immense wagon trains, and listening to the thunder of Thomas's magnificent fight.

About the middle of the afternoon a bustle and excitement was noticeable in the town. Orderlies galloped hurriedly about; staff officers appeared and assumed authority; stragglers were picked up by armed patrols and marched away. Order seemed to spring up all around as if by magic. Soon it was whispered around that the commanding General had arrived. After awhile shouts and cheers were audible away out on the plain toward the mountain, and then along the lines nearer and nearer, until we could see the commotion at the river above us. "Old Rosey" was there, sure enough; it was his presence that brought order and enthusiasm out of chaos and despair. Later in the afternoon the fact became known that Generals McCook and Crittenden had also arrived from the front, followed by depressing rumors of their corps having been cut to pieces.*

That Sunday night is one of fearful memory. Where was the army? what was to be our fate? were the queries in every mind. The reports brought in by teamsters and others led us to fear the worst.

All night long the wagons and stragglers poured in on the different roads—the stragglers being promptly put out in the trenches, where,

> " By the struggling moonbeam's misty light,
> And the lanterns dimly burning,"

they vigorously plied the pick and shovel, under the direction of Rosecrans and his engineers, throwing up a line of works from the mountain's base to the river.

On Monday we had a little diversion. We received orders to climb Lookout-Mountain, scout the approaches to the

---

*The reader will understand that this chapter records only the movements made and scenes witnessed by the Company (L) to which the author belonged. The main portion of the regiment, under Colonel Wm. J. Palmer, remained on the field during both days of the battle rendering important service as couriers, orderlies, and escort. When Davis's division gave way on Sunday, the Anderson Cavalry had the delicate and difficult task of arresting the flying troops. An eye-witness of the scene (Sergt. Wm. Gable, Co. I) relates that in the height of the tumult and confusion Major General McCook and staff rode up; and to a question from an officer of the Anderson Cavalry as to where he should place his men to be most effective, the General replied, excitedly: "Back, back to Chattanooga—every man must get back to Chattanooga." And soon after away went the commander of the 20th Corps, obeying his own injunction. But Old Roman Thomas did not th'nk it necessary to get back so hurriedly!

7

summit, and guard the signal station there, the flags of of which we could plainly see from over the river. It was highly important to retain so splendid a position as long as possible in view of the occupation of Chattanooga by our forces, and the consequent following up of Bragg's, who would thus place himself directly under our telescopes

Leaving our wagons, therefore—virtually cutting loose from our base—we re-crossed the river and made our way over the plain, now tumbled up into formidable earth-works, to the mountain. As an illustration of the growing scarcity of hard-tack, it may be stated that in passing through the town some keen-scented trooper found a negro man with a lot of musty ginger-bread to sell, in pieces no larger than a man's hand, at fifty cents each, Federal currency. His stock, some dozen pieces, was bought out in less time than I have taken to tell it.

But O! that weary, panting, exhausting ascent of Lookout Mountain! leading, almost dragging, our weak-legged Rosinantes; sinking down in our tracks every ten minutes to rest and gasp for breath. Not the magnificent views that stretched away below us, nor the significant boom of artillery that occasionally came up, nor the portentous clouds of dust that hovered over the Mission Hills, could rouse our senses from the lethargy of fatigue. Mechanically we toiled onward and upward; and when at length, about noon, the upper level was reached, the entire party, biped and quadruped, sank gasping and quivering upon the rocks.

Three hours later we had recovered sufficiently to drag ourselves up the plateau to Summertown. This was a handsome little place, a noted resort of the chivalry, and contained an immense hotel, into which we incontinently bestowed ourselves. Evidences of hasty evacuation were visible on all hands; but we found scattered through the big rooms almost every physical and œsthetical comfort commonly kept in hotels. I except the very essential one of food. Pianos, sofas, chairs, bedsteads and feather beds, statuettes, books, crockery-ware and cooking utensils— these we found in abundance; but not a scrap of any thing eatable.

The village was utterly deserted, save by two women and some children, who peered from the windows in great alarm. Finding, however, that we made no attempt to molest them, or to appropriate their little store of corn meal, they soon became friendly and communicative.

The signal officer, with his corps of three men, was stationed on a projecting rock, a little distance above the hotel. The position afforded a visual sweep that seemed to take in the entire South.

We remained here only a little while. The roads were to be picketed, forage must be found. Leaving a detachment at the station, we groped our way through the pitchy darkness for six or seven miles down the ridge. Not a living thing was encountered in our travels, except a sleeping cavalryman and his horse, whom we found at midnight under a tree in the woods, and at first took for a napping rebel picket; but he turned out to be a member of the 12th Kentucky (Union) Cavalry, which regiment had been cut to pieces in the valley.

For the rest of the night we picketed the roads leading up from east to south. It was my fate to be placed at the furthest outpost on the southern road, over a mile from the reserve. By this road it was almost certain the enemy would make his approach—whether that night or not was the only question. O the interminable length of those " wee sma' hours," when Birney and I stood to horse just inside the thickets, cold, weary, half starved, and half asleep, awaiting the tardy dawn ! We expected every moment to hear the sound of hostile hoofs. It seemed as if daylight would never come. Nor was it the least part of our misery to see our poor brute companions gnawing the bushes around them in the extremity of their hunger.

When at last the welcome sun gilded the tree tops above us, and brought a recall, we returned sore and famished to our no less suffering comrades.

Returning to Summertown we found that the army had fallen back during the night, and was occupying the hastily built works around Chattanooga. It was probable, therefore, that the rebel Cavalry were already swarming around the mountain, cutting off our escape. Starvation or captivity —the alternatives seemed about equal. So we looked upon them with the stolidity of veterans, thrumming the pianos and lounging on the sofas and beds, trusting in Heaven and Rosecrans for deliverance.

On this day—the 22d of September—it was our good fortune to witness scenes, which, as viewed by us, have probably had no parallel in this war, and which rendered us for a time oblivious of danger and physical privations, albeit "the difficult air of the mountain top" increased the keenness of our hunger.

The day was calm and clear. From the overhanging cliffs we beheld the country mapped out beneath us for fifty miles around. As far as the eye could separate them, appeared an agreeable diversity of wooded ridge and open plain, bathed in the sunlight, rich in the blended variety of early autumn tints, through which from east to west the silvery stream of the Tennessee wound its crooked way. In the dim distance, on every hand, the hills and mountain spurs rolled away in purple billows to the horizon. Far off in the south-east the air still looked heavy with the smoke and dust of battle. Directly under our feet, as it seemed, lay Chattanooga,—an infinitesimal "city"—encircled by yellow lines of, earthworks, which extended unbrokenly from the mountain to the river. An inner circle of dark blue was still more apparent, from which the bayonets and colors gleamed in the sunlight—as though visibly tipped with the glory of as gallant a fight as any in history.

In rear of the lines the plain and town were dotted with innumerable "dog tents," looking at that distance like clusters of snow-balls. Over the river were vast parks of wagons, covering many acres, but at our height apparently spread over a few square yards. Still through the town, and over the thread-like pontoons, crawled long lines of diminutive white wagons, each one a Queen Mab's chariot,

"Drawn by a team of little atomies!"

That was an absorbed group that watched these scenes from Lookout Mountain. The signal officer kept his eye glued to his glass, which was trained upon the approaches to Chattanooga. He evidently expected the appearance of the rebels. Every eye around him was on the watch, every tongue silent. Soon the atmosphere beyond the Mission ridges grew hazy, and small clouds of dust rose slowly in the air. The excitement of our party at this moment was intense, but the stillness was so profound that the music of a band in Chattanooga was distinctly heard. Suddenly the signal officer slapped his knee and exclaimed quietly, "They are coming" ! at the same time giving some orders to his flagmen, who, screened by a thicket from the enemy's observation, waved their colors vigorously. Sure enough, when a puff of wind lifted the hazy vail in the distance there appeared small squads of horsemen coming cautiously forward on the Rossville and Dry Valley roads. Behind them other distinct clouds arose, from which larger bodies of cavalry emerged. Simultaneously, on another road further south, leading over the ridges beneath us, like a scene occurred, and I was able to distinguish the flags of these parties, and the colors of their horses. In a moment more little puffs of white smoke floating up from the roads and the trees, followed by the faint rattle of carbines, told that the pickets of the two armies had met again. And now while we gazed, long, gray columns of infantry and strings of artillery appeared upon the roads, barely distinguishable from the clouds of dust which they created. One gun was seen to move into an open field, between the two main columns of the enemy. Immediately thereafter a dull red flash came from the spot, followed by the unmistakeable crash of a Napoleon gun. Instantly our guns replied; and for a little while there was a beautiful artillery skirmish, every shot being plainly visible to us. The rebel gun was the first to be silent, and we saw it withdrawn.

All this while, and for the rest of the day, the rebel columns continued to crawl over the hills like a swarm of insects, settling down into the fields, or disappearing in the woods. As their lines extended and developed ours, the skirmishing became sharper and heavier, rising at times into the genuine roar of battle.

Who of the few that saw that sight can ever forget it? Were we to witness a still grander scene, an assault upon our works? If Bragg had any such notion at five o'clock —at which time the skirmishing was heaviest—his purpose was changed before night-fall. For as the mighty shadow of Lookout crept over the two armies, the fight dwindled away to a straggling picket fire, and here and there along both lines the bright twinkle of bivouac fires appeared, emerging with the stars and apparently in similar numbers. Two parallel semi-circles of blinking light, broken in spots by intervening woods, marked the opposing armies.

I reclined on a ledge of rock for some hours, looking off
upon this grand historic scene, listening to the rifle cracks,
and between them to the confused murmur of the camps,
the music of the bands, and the occasional cheer of some
enthusiastic regiment.

But the night dews were gathering heavily; so taking
one last comprehensive look, I reluctantly withdrew to the
hotel, where I bestowed myself between two feather beds—
not without apprehension lest, before morning, a rebel sabre
or bayonet should pin me there forever.

The sun was high when I got up—for no early bugle
was allowed to wake the mountain echoes. Looking over
the rocks, the blue army and the gray still confronted each
other, but in quiet. Both had, as if by tacit consent, ceased
for awhile to murder pickets. But the Union colors and
steel gleamed out proudly along the yellow works, and
bands of music filled the air with defiant notes.

They were ready for Bragg's assault.

But Bragg was settling quietly down into his memorable
seige, confident of receiving in due time the surrender of
an emaciated and starving army. Things looked well for
the Confederacy, in this quarter. Nor was the Federal
army without those who feared that our successes at
Vicksburg and Gettysburg were about to be balanced.

It now became necessary to look more closely to our own
safety. The rebels swarmed about the eastern base of the
mountain; their outposts were perhaps pushed half-way to
the summit, on the only road by which we could descend.
It was not probable that they would permit another day to
pass before feeling their way to our retreat. Our provisions were absolutely gone; horses and men were ravenous.

To attempt cutting our way through, even if we had
fed on capons and oats, would have been folly. A party
went down the ridge on the western side in hopes of find-

ing a descent into Lookout valley. The boys might have climbed or tumbled down, but there was no visible foothold for a horse, except at the Gaps, many miles below.

The fatigues and privations we had undergone produced a feeling of indifference as to our fate; and as we returned, slowly and despairingly, to Summertown, every mind was made up to submit with a stolid grace to (apparently) inevitable capture. But, reaching the signal station, we found a stranger there—externally a butternut, tho' really a noted Federal scout. He was a young man, and for years had passed almost daily through perils that would have whitened the hair of ordinary men; yet he was as fresh as a daisy, quick, but quiet and collected, with clear steel-gray eyes that seemed the very incarnation of cool courage.

Our friend was fresh from the rebel lines, which he reported in close proximity. A council of war was held, and the situation was thoroughly canvassed. The scout volunteered to conduct us down by a route known only to himself, and that extremely hazardous. We felt that it must indeed be so when he asked for a suit of our regimentals—for if found by the enemy leading us in his butternut jeans he would have swung for it to the first tree. We assorted a suit for him from the contents of our saddlebags, and he was soon metamorphosed into a Federal trooper.

At noon, all things being ready—pistols and carbines carefully loaded and capped—we followed our guide down the road by which we had ascended, pulling our skeleton beasts after us. The gloomy and silent woods below were thoroughly scanned as we proceeded, lest a lurking ambush should start up around. Our footsteps in the dust sounded painfully loud. The occasional stumbling of a horse or bouncing of a loosened stone down the declivity, startled the echoes like a rebel yell. After traveling thus for a half hour or so, we stopped at a sudden sign from the scout He went on down the road some distance, and laid himself flat on the road-side, with his ear to the ground; then rising, he seemed to examine the trees. His actions were as intelligible as a pantomine. We all correctly understood them to mean that the enemy was but a little way below us and it was not safe to go any further. We now followed him away from the road; directly northward along the steep mountain side. Climbing over boulders, rocks and fallen timber; wading knee-deep through fallen leaves and twigs; scrambling through bushes and thorn-trees—such was the exhausting labyrinth through which we toiled for hours. It was with incredible difficulty that our miserable beasts were dragged and cuffed along. There was no sign of a path, save to the practised eye of the guide, to whom every rock and tree was no doubt familiar.

We now heard the renewed picket skirmish, which sounded as though but a little way below us, and might at any moment burst into view.

Suddenly the loud "Halt"! of a picket echoed and re-echoed around. Reins were dropped in trepidation, and carbines were clutched—but only for an instant. There before us, not twenty yards away, a tall *blue*-coated soldier stepped out from behind a tree. Safe at last! was the exclamation of hearts that had stood still for two hours.

Sliding down the steep paths to Chatanooga creek, which we crossed under the rail road bridge, we made an entry once more into Chattanooga, a happy, but sore and starving troop.

The morning after these adventures revealed the rebel colors floating from the top of Lookout Mountain!

APPENDIX.

An Account of the Mutiny in the Anderson Cavalry, at

Nashville, Tenn., December, 1862.

To THE AUTHOR OF THE "LEAVES":

My Dear Captain:—At the repeated requests of many of those most interested I avail myself of the opportunity you offer me to publish a statement of the troubles in the Anderson Cavalry known as the "Mutiny." Such a statement has, I believe, long been expected from me on account of the peculiar position I occupied in the organization for some time previous to and following the outbreak. I was the only member of the regiment who received a commission in it until after the troubles had subsided; and in my capacity as Commissary and acting Quartermaster I was brought into intimate contact with all parties. I was also placed in command of the camp of the mutineers until their arrest by the authorities; made it a part of my duty to be among them as much as possible during their confinement; and was placed in command of them again when they were removed to the barracks preparatory to re-organization.

It is never too late to correct wrong impressions. I have always considered it due to the men, to their friends, and to history, that some attempt should be made to clear away the doubt that still, with many people, obscures the fair fame of the regiment. If my statement, offered, as I have said, in compliance with repeated requests, shall tend at this late day to re-open old sores and to revive unpleasant controversies, no one will regret that result more than myself; but while I shall endeavor in this brief narrative to maintain an impartiality that cannot be misrepresented nor misunderstood, I propose to write what I believe to be the truth, holding myself, of course, responsible for all my statements, and ready if called upon either to reiterate or retract, according as I am confirmed of truth or convinced of error.

The *personnel* of the regiment caused it to be regarded with jealousy at the start. Enlisting was then (1862) no longer looked upon as going on "Governor Seward's three months' picnic." There were many young men, who, while anxious to enter the service, were averse to forced association with a class that frequently composed our eastern regiments. Captain Palmer's shrewd knowledge of human nature led him to sieze the opportunity for so golden a harvest. He obtained authority to raise a battalion of 400 men, to be strictly confined to the class of young men above referred to; and then was seen the singular military spectacle of the recruit presenting himself for enlistment with letters of recommendation from reputable parties, which might or might not obtain his admission to the surgeon. The success of the plan was so speedy and immense that after the battalion had been obtained, the recruiting went on unchecked, and in the course of a month there was gathered in camp at Carlisle a *regiment* of men, the like of which, I venture to say, never before entered into the composition of an army.

But this great success was one of the principal sources of the subsequent troubles. It is impossible for one man to organize, equip, and discipline a regiment; yet Captain Palmer attempted it alone, though afterward aided by an officer who was an invalid. This officer being in charge of camp, was in the habit—possibly from indisposition—of leaving the command every night to a private of another organization. Indeed for a period of about two months this large body of men was left almost alone, without even a non-commissioned officer in camp.

Beginning their military life under such neglect, with accommodations more wretched and scanty than they ever afterwards possessed in the field, with arms and accoutrements that were the condemned refuse of the Indian wars, it is not strange that the spirit of discontent should have started up among these men. And it is a splendid proof of their intelligence and patriotism that,notwithstanding these depressing influences, there was no disorder in the camp, and but three desertions.

I have said that the command was often left "to a private of another organization." This introduces a subject which I approach with regret, but cannot avoid, as it involves the *chief* cause of the subsequent disorders. The organization alluded to was called the *"Anderson Troop,"* a company of 100 men selected from all parts of the state, recruited for and serving as the body-guard or escort of Maj. Gen. Buell. They had been officially reported to be the finest body of men in the western army.

Many people supposed then—and do still—that this *"Anderson Troop"* and the "ANDERSON CAVALRY" were one and the same. So, indeed, they should have been, and so, apparently, was the original intention, for there was a general understanding among the members of the CAVALRY that the "Old Troop" (as the body-guard was called) was to be company "A" of the new regiment; in fact the first company of the CAVALRY, in its original organization, was always designated as "B."

But it soon became apparent that the interests of these two bodies were not identical. What arrangements or promises Captain Palmer made with the gentlemen of the body-guard have never transpired; but it speedily became obvious to the CAVALRY that there was a scrambling rivalry among the former for the commissions in the new regiment. The rivalry between those who had been detailed to assist in the recruiting and those who still remained in the field, ran very high. Every man of them looked upon himself as the heir apparent to a commission. I say this in no disparagement of their ambition, which was natural and laudable; but they made the fatal mistake, in thus seeking their own promotion, of assuming that the commissions belonged only to them—that the regiment was their exclusive property by virtue of their belonging to the body-guard—that the men whom they assumed to command "had no rights which they were bound to respect." As there was scarcely a man in the CAVALRY who would not have honored a commission, they, as may be supposed, looked upon this appropriation of themselves with no great meekness. Witnessing the rivalry, suffering from the consequent delays and neglect, was it unreasonable that the men began at length to feel that they had been en- listed not for the good of the service, but for the purpose of furnishing commissions to a body of men who looked upon them as their aristocratic right? Could they fail to trace out comparisons between this state of affairs, with their consequent ill condition and prospects, and what might have existed if their organization had been properly and speedily effected in accordance with regulations?

The consequence was that there arose in the regiment a wide-spread distrust of Captain Palmer and the body guard. Although the former was unknown to and had never been seen by most of the men, yet, owing to the state

8

of things above narrated, all his measures and proposals looking to the special service for which the regiment had been raised were regarded with suspicion, and even met with opposition and rebuff.

Here let me say in justice to Captain Palmer that when he became cognizant of the manner in which the camp at Carlisle had been mismanaged and neglected, he expressed strong displeasure. I am willing to believe that he had not anticipated, and is still unconscious of, the extent and bitterness of the scramble for power among his old subordinates.

To show the disordered state of affairs at this time, I will here state a few facts. The Captain being in Rebel hands, and the Lieutenant being sick, the command of the CAVALRY devolved upon the Orderly Sergeant of the body-guard. By his order I took possession of such papers relating to the Commissary and Quartermaster departments as could be found; but it was impossible to tell what requisitions had been made, or how and upon whom they had been drawn. Investigations, laborious and protracted, revealed that a portion of our stores had been sent to the front, and had been in possession of the enemy. Special inquiries were made at the State capital, and the officer in charge of the Quartermaster's department there said "that he did not know that we had any right to draw through the State authorities, as neither himself nor the Adjutant-General of the State knew whether we belonged to the State or to the General Government."

Governor Curtin said "that he had been trying to get control of the regiment, but had not succeeded; that the whole matter of the previous requisitions had been hurried through in a very loose way, and that it was now time to come down to some system about it; that if he had control of us, things would be brought up with a round turn."

I also found that there was not even a roster of the regiment, and I had one prepared in the camp for my own use, showing an aggregate of 994 enlisted men. To command this full regiment there were less than a dozen officers commissioned at Carlisle.

Putting all these facts together—and many minor ones which the limits of this letter exclude—the men of the CAVALRY began to fear that there had been no authority to recruit more than the one battalion originally proposed; that the true cause of the disorganized condition of the command was the absence of authority to organize. And yet such was the devotion of these men to themselves as a body, such the strength of their hope in the future, that when, after the campaign of Antietam, a great majority of them were furloughed in the loosest way—some even verbally—there was not a single desertion.

A little more evidence of the bad condition of things. Before the gentlemen of the body-guard had received their commissions, the duty of drilling the CAVALRY was performed by Sergeants and Corporals of the barracks; but now, after being fully clothed with the long looked for authority, the new officers continued to permit their men to be drilled as before, and did not personally attend to their duties. This abuse became at last so flagrant that Captain Ward, who was then commanding, found no other remedy than to remove the camp from the vicinity of the barracks to the other side of the town.

Having been appointed acting Q. M. Sergeant (as a "temporary arrangement")* and orders read that I was

---

* Every Anderson Cavalryman will understand the application of this phrase; but to others some explanation is necessary. Be it known, then, that for a long time the orders issued to the regiment at Carlisle always bore these words as a preface or appendix, qualifying appointments, regulations, details, etc., as so many "temporary arrangements."

to be obeyed and respected accordingly, I went to the barracks to attend to my duties as usual (having done so for two months) when I found a member of the body-guard there before me. He was there by orders from the Lt. Colonel of the regiment (late Lieutenant of the body-guard.) Notwithstanding my long occupation of the position, being only a private of the CAVALRY it was not considered worth while to give me any official notice of having been relieved.

On my way back to camp I was overtaken by an orderly with orders to me to report immediately to Captain Hastings, U. S. A., commanding the barracks and Post. He said to me: "I have sent marching orders to your camp, but no notice has been taken of them. When will you leave?"

I told the Captain that I was only a private soldier; had been up to that evening, acting as Quartermaster, but finding another attending to the duties of that position, supposed I has been relieved.

"I dont know," said he, " what your position is, nor can I understand how your regiment is organized; but I learn from my subordinates that you are the only executive officer in the command who can give me the necessary information."

While Captain Hastings was still talking to me the Lieut.-Colonel of the CAVALRY was announced. He had been a sergeant at these barracks, under the veteran who still commanded there, and was subsequently (as has been stated) Lieutenant of Buell's body-guard. As he entered

---

What the *permanent* arrangements were intended to be will probably never be made known. This unhappy designation came at length to be regarded as fatally bound up with the affairs of the organization, and passed into a regimental proverb.

in full uniform the Captain U. S. A. arose and saluted his
superior officer. Here, then, was the explanation of the
indifference to the marching orders, of which the Captain
had just complained! I left the room feeling that the
rivalry between the regiment and the regulars of the
barracks should not be charged entirely on the privates of
the regiment. Notwithstanding this rival feeling, let me
here state, the regiment was indebted to Captain Hastings
and Ordnance Sergeant Furay for many comforts which
they could not otherwise have obtained.

For some reason or other my commission as Commissary
was withheld until the regiment was about to move. As
it then became apparent that some one would be compelled
to assume the responsibility of providing for the troops
while *en route*, I was notified on the day previous to the
departure that I would be commissioned. There were
no haversacks for the men, no provisions but for one day.
I waited anxiously for instructions until after dark, and
then, as none came, made bold to report to the commanding officer for orders. I received only severe censure for
intruding upon him after "office hours!" Determined,
however, that the responsibility of such neglect should have
no chance to fall upon me, I took private conveyance
early next morning to Harrisburg, was mustered in, and
secured the necessary supplies, with which I joined the
regiment as it passed through.

I have been circumstantial in the foregoing, because in
no other way could I show in its true light the utter confusion and want of system in the organization.

During the transportation of the regiment to the West
the growing dissatisfaction was lulled by change of scene
by enthusiastic welcome along the route, and by hope of
better times when our destination should be reached.
Throughout that long ride to Louisville these men pre-

served decorum, though unguarded and virtually without officers—for the latter chose to carry their aristocratic ideas so far as to remain together and let their men look out for themselves. That many stragglers dropped off along the route, and did not return for weeks, is not surprising; but that they returned at all voluntarily, when desertion was so easy and the chances of inquiry doubtful— and, more than all—in the face of the disorganization and discontent of their comrades, proves that they possessed a wonderful innate sense of duty, and a no less wonderful hope.

As soon as we had got settled in camp at Louisville the unhappy internal condition of affairs again became apparent. It had been expected by the CAVALRY, as intimated heretofore, that the body-guard would be transferred to the regiment at Louisville as company "A," and that they would, therefore, receive their full complement of officers, and complete their organization. We found here, however, only the senior Major. But the regiment was not to be without acting officers—" temporary arrangements "—as was soon demonstrated. Members of the body-guard, on leaves of absence, would visit their commissioned comrades in the camp, and while remaining be invested by their friends with the authority to wear the scarf and act as officers of the day or of the guard. The baker of the body-guard, a foreigner who could scarcely speak English, often assumed such *role*. All this, the reader will understand, from no other reason than that they belonged to the "Old Troop," and were therefore (as they believed) the legitimate heirs of the power they assumed. Those who can conceive the pride a true soldier takes in his organization will not fail to see the exasperating tendencies of such assumptions—such unauthorized handing over of a regiment bodily to privates of a different organization.

Nor was there any improvement in other internal affairs. A constant conflict of authority was going on between the Lieut.-Colonel Commanding and the Majors—the latter energetically endeavoring to equip the command and put it into service. This clash of authority found a scape-goat in me, as it had many times before. Thus, although I had been relieved from duty at Carlisle as Acting Quartermaster, (by finding another in the place, as stated) yet here I was constantly receiving orders from the Majors to turn in surplus stores, etc., and was as constantly threatened by the Lieut.-Colonel with arrest if I did so—he being unwilling to sign even an invoice for stores turned in.

These complications could not do otherwise than increase the uneasiness and discontent in the regiment. The long suppressed feelings of the men began to find voice. They took counsel among themselves in their messes, and in groups by the evening fires, and afterwards in meetings *en masse* that shadowed the coming storm. Letters were drawn up and sent to the Secretary of War and the Governor of their State, setting forth the nature of their grievances, and entreating for the good of the service that a regular organization might be vouchsafed them. Some of the men, having no faith in the virtue of these appeals, and knowing full well the determined spirit of their comrades, concluded that the organization was already on its last legs, and left it for their homes, intending to enter other regiments. These absentees, however, returned when it was officially announced that the CAVALRY was being re-organized at Murfreesboro.

At this time the men had formed the determination, and had notified the officers of it, not to march beyond Nashville without a proper organization. So well aware were the Majors of this intention that they contemplated asking permission to cross the country into East Tennessee and burn the rail-road bridge at Strawberry Plains. They hoped by activity in the field, and the reputation which such an achievement would have won, to inspirit the men and divert their thoughts from the unhappy condition of regimental affairs. I know this to be a fact; for, having formerly lived in East Tennessee, the Majors frequently consulted me, while on the march to Nashville, about their project, and also discussed the condition of the command, and the probable end of the troubles. It is to be regretted that the scheme they proposed was not carried out.

After leaving Louisville—the Lieut. Colonel following the main body with two companies—Major Rosengarten requested me to take temporary possession of the Quartermaster's department, the gentleman of the body-guard who had relieved me of that trust at Carlisle being (as stated heretofore) only a private and unauthorized to sign receipts. As it was urged upon me by both Majors as tending to allay the dissatisfaction in the regiment, as well as in the light of a personal favor to them, I accepted until we should reach Nashville, where a Quartermaster was supposed to be awaiting us.

I found that no proper blanks had been provided, and not half the transportation that was allowable; and such wagons as we had were mostly loaded with surplus stores which should have been left at Louisville. This was the cause of much unnecessary trouble and suffering. Not being able to carry subsistence, we were compelled to keep up a constant scouring of a country that had already been well gleaned by two great armies.

We reached Nashville on the evening of the 24th December. The regiment was halted in the streets while I rode off, by Major Rosengarten's orders, to report our arrival to the commanding General, whom I found at a council of of war with a room-full of Generals. My orders were to report to him in person, and to do so I was compelled to push by guards and elbow Major Generals. General Rosecrans received me courteously and gave some instructions to Col. Goddard A. A. G., who directed me where the command was to locate, and ordered also that we should report to the Chief of Cavalry. While the regiment was going to camp, which was near Stanley's head-quarters, Major Rosengarten sent me off to report to that General. I did so, and at the same time made a requisition for forage, and got the promise of it in the morning.

I also found that the ANDERSON CAVALRY had been brigaded with some other new regiments.

This fact has been considered by many as the pretext for the outbreak; and, indeed, having been recruited as an independent organization, it is only natural that the brigading should have increased the discontent among the men. But I have already shown that the determination of the majority not to march beyond Nashville without being efficiently officered, was formed at Louisville, as the result of causes hereinbefore mentioned, and that it was well known to the officers. As an instance of this, and as showing the quiet spirit that actuated the men, I will state that on coming to camp that night, before the fact of the brigading was known to any one in the regiment but myself, I heard one of the best sergeants say to his horse, while unsaddling, "*There, that is the last time it goes on your back until these difficulties are settled.*"

I reported this incident to the Major, who appreciated its significance, and talked with me long and anxiously as to the probable action of the men.

There is no reason to suppose that if the regiment had been properly organized and officered, a single man would have mutinied. Let me here say that I am attempting no apology for the outbreak. I opposed it from the start, and was the first (and for a time the *only*) officer who went personally among the men to dissuade them from such action. I always regarded their conduct as the efforts of courageous, high-spirited, but impetuous men to obtain an effective military organization; smarting under the neglect and confusion arising from the squabbles of another organization to obtain exclusive control of them; and fearful lest the splendid prospects with which they enlisted should fizzle away under incapacity and mismanagement: the whole arising, as they could not fail to see, from the irregular, irresponsible, and "temporary" manner in which they had originally been recruited and organized.

As to the charge of cowardice, which some stay-at-home and detailed-in-the-rear warriors have had the insolence to advance, I consider it unworthy of aught but simple mention as a part of the history of the event.

Shortly after going into camp, orders were brought to march the regiment at an early hour in the morning (Christmas). The Major handed me the despatch, and I told him I did not see how it was possible to move so soon, without a single ration of forage or subsistence, or a round of ammunition, all which would have to be drawn on the morrow. The horses had not been fed for more than a day, and had had but little for four days.

"Well," said he, "the orders are peremptory, and you must try to get these things to-night."

Unfortunately, no one had been left to guide the wagons to camp, and but three succeeded in reaching us; these three, too, were deserted by their drivers, who had returned to their companies, having previously obtained the permission of their officers to do so when the regiment should arrive at Nashville. It took me until near morning to get volunteer drivers, find the Commissary's and get provisions; but we still had no forage nor ammunition. About day-break, the marching orders were countermanded, and instead of receiving the promised forage orders were sent to us for a train and guard to go after it beyond the lines. Owing to miserable management this party was driven back by the rebels, with the loss of one of our men.

This incident helped to deepen the discontent, and was regarded by the men as sadly confirmatory of their worst fears that "temporary arrangements" would bring upon them only disaster and disgrace.

All this day the regiment remained quietly in camp, but during the day sent a committee to wait upon the Lieut. Colonel (who had arrived and was commanding), stating to him their purpose not to leave that camp until properly organized. This notification seemed to produce no impression upon the commander, and the swelling tide of the mutiny was allowed to take its course. I know not what occurred at this interview, but to illustrate some of the characteristics of the officer referred to, I will state in detail the difficulties and delays which I had to go through that very day to obtain his signature to the requisition necessary to procure ammunition.

Presenting the document to him, I reminded him of the urgency of the matter, and asked his immediate approval. He said he would send it to me. After waiting some time I sent an orderly for it, and it was returned *unsigned.* In a sort of blind hope I took it to the ordnance officer, but he very properly refused to issue on it without approval. I returned it to the Lieut. Colonel with a written request that he would sign it immediately; his answer was that he would *attend to it*. Waiting awhile again, I went to head-quarters and found the envelope open, but the requisition *still unsigned*. I ventured then to carry it in person to the Majors, but they declined to approve it as they were not in command. I then addressed the requisition "*To whoever is in command of the Anderson Cavalry*," and sent it to the head-quarters tent. Not receiving it back, I went to the tent again, found the document on his table, and handed it to him. Said he: "This is insolent!" I insisted that he should sign the paper, and he again said he would *send it to me*. But I remained there for a considerable time, and the requisition was still unapproved. In despair I took it from the table and was about to leave the tent, when he asked what I was going to do. I answered that I was not willing to be held responsible for the absence of ammunition, and that I was going to report to Gen. Stanley his refusal to approve the necessary papers.

He then took and signed it! Nearly an entire day was consumed in these efforts, and it was after dark before I secured the ammunition.

In anticipation of the march in the morning (orders to that effect having been received), I was detailed to remain in charge of the camp, with a guard and the sick. The usual confusion of things was exhibited even in this, for I received but two of the details, and found it impossible to make a correct roll of those who remained with me by orders.

The memorable morning—December 26—arrived. About 7 o'clock orders came to march; but, although the usual early *reveille* had been sounded, the marching orders were followed by no "Officers' Call," no "Boots and Saddles," no formal intimation whatever to the men that they were expected to go anywhere. Authority in the regiment, always confused and irregular, was now utterly paralyzed, and the outbreak received the strongest encouragement by meeting with no official opposition.

It soon became manifest that but a few were preparing to march. Only one company entire (L)* saddled up, when it became known that the command had been ordered off.

Meeting Major Rosengarten, we rode together outside of camp, and talked the situation over. He was much vexed at the mismanagement of affairs, and the lamentable result, and, as if in despair, rode off to head-quarters to persuade Gen. Rosecrans to countermand the order of march for the Anderson Cavalry, in hope of gaining time for a speedy settlement of the difficulties. In this request he was joined by Gen. Mitchell, Commanding District, who was also aware of the condition of the regiment, and stated further that he would need their assistance to convoy trains to and from the front. But the Commanding General deemed it best not to grant the request.

Returning to camp I found no further preparations making, but the arms were stacked in the company streets, and the men remained quietly in their quarters. The officers were gathered at head-quarters, clanned together as usual, discussing the situation, and, no doubt, ready to *follow* such of their men as would decide to go. I heard one of the Captains say "that he hoped the men would remain firm, and that he would be glad of an opportunity to go with the boys"—meaning the body-guard. Going among the men of this officer's company, I had no great difficulty in persuading most of them to saddle up, and I

---

* Excepting one member of it.

reported to their Captain that his men were going. The strongest argument I used with these men was that there certainly would be a battle.

Another officer requested me to use my efforts with his company, which I gladly did; but when I had got so far as to consider my mission accomplished, up rides an orderly from head-quarters, a member of the body-guard, who proceeded to tell what he knew. His opinion of the military situation was different from mine, for he assured his hearers that there certainly would *not* be a battle, that it was "merely the forward movement of a campaign"; and that they must not allow themselves to be diverted from their purpose by other statements, &c., &c. Other orderlies from head-quarters (members of the body-guard) frequently passed through the camp reiterating these assurances, and advising the CAVALRY to stand firm.

Major Ward, who was sick and dispirited, said to my entreaty that he would remain in camp: "No, I will go with the boys that go into this battle, and then resign, for I am not willing to see such men so shamefully treated.

I am very careful in reporting the actions and words of the deceased Majors at this time, as there is no one but myself to mention them.

After the three hundred had gone—some of them, including the two Majors, never to return alive—I personally reported the state of affairs to Gen. Mitchell. He censured me severely, in the warmth of his feeling, saying that experience had proved that the inefficiency of officers was the cause of all the troubles in volunteer . regiments.

During the next few days the camp was visited by many officers, soldiers, and citizens, all anxious to see the "mutineers." Most of these visitors advised the men to maintain their position. The quiet and orderly conduct of all—guarding their own camp, &c.,—seemed to astonish observers, who probably expected to find a turbulent and noisy crew, held in subjection by the bayonet. This impression was also shared by the authorities, for I was twice offered a guard for personal protection! Members of the regiment, especially those who remained at camp, will smile at this evidence of the desperate reputation which they had unconsciously acquired. As for myself I need hardly say that I never felt safer in my life than I did amongst these terrible fellows, although I was aware of being very unpopular with them.

The bulk of the rations drawn for the regiment having gone to the front with the three hundred, those men who remained were compelled, (after sharing the provisions that had been retained for the guards, &c.) to forage for subsistence in the best way they could. For the horses they were glad to dig up the refuse corn from the mud at the late site of the wagon parks; and as for the men themselves, I need only state that I—though a Commissary and acting Quartermaster, positions wherein one is supposed always to be able to look out for self—was very glad to purchase from an Irish laborer in the Q. M. D. the cold remnants of his dinner. But the men stood it bravely, accepting with a good grace the consequences of their defection.

During this time I did all that my poor efforts could do to reason with them, speaking to them individually and collectively; but the only result of my endeavors seemed to be that I was looked upon as *crazy* on the subject—an impression which obtains among some of them to this day!

On the 29th December, a Captain came to camp, having been out with a squad of the men to secure and bury the body of our comrade who had been killed on Christmas morning. I turned over the camp to this officer, and he succeeded in obtaining about 30 men to go with him to the front. Before starting that way, I accompanied him to Gen. Mitchell, to whom he reported the refusal of the rest of the command to march with him. At this interview with Gen. Mitchell, Gen. Morgan, commanding the Post, being present, they both declared it to be their purpose to fire upon the mutineers if still persistent in their disobedience.

Accordingly on the next day (30th), Gen. Morgan marched a regiment of infantry and one of cavalry to the camp, and surrounded it. He then sent a message to the men that he wished to address them. Immediately, with true soldierly spirit, they went to their quarters and equipped themselves as for dress parade, but without arms; marched out by companies and formed regimental front with a precision and celerity that made a visible impression on the troops that surrounded them.

Gen. Morgan then ordered his men to load, after which he read his orders, and asked the CAVALRY if they still refused to march. A few stepped to the front, one after another, and replied, briefly referring to their defective organization; to the long suffering and forbearance with which from Carlisle to that place they had withstood the consequent neglect and abuse; to their appeals to the Governor of their State and to the General Government, which had met with no attention. They had not made this stand out of fear of the enemy, for they were ready to meet death there, if need be, at the hands of their friends.

The General replied in substance: "Of your organization or history I know nothing, nor is it my business to consider either. You are soldiers, sworn to obey the orders of your superiors. I also am a soldier, and am here under orders to compel your obedience. I do not wish to use the force with which I have been sent here, but I should be in mutiny like yourselves if I refused to obey my orders."

He then announced that he would allow them five minutes to come to decision.

It was a remarkable scene. Here were less than 500 men, standing shoulder to shoulder, silent and determined; without arms, but strong in their conviction of right; facing two regiments that might in a few moments more cut them to pieces. The five minutes grace were passing away—the last one had come, the most trying moment or my life. I begged the General to grant five minutes more, and asked his permission to go amongst the men. I appealed to them by every consideration that could touch the heads or hearts of people; but the only result of my efforts was that some of my own guards joined the ranks to share the fate of their comrades.

General Morgan was a man of tact as well as of feeling. He assured the CAVALRY that, after all, their wishes and his orders were about the same; that his desire was to lead them to Gen. Rosecrans, who would see, he doubted not, that they were at once properly organized. This proposition had the desired effect. The men saddled up with alacrity; indeed, so universal was the desire to go to the front, and so inspiring the hope that something at last would be done for the regiment, that I was compelled to threaten some of my own detachment with arrest to prevent them from going.

Gen. Morgan detailed Col. Woods, of the Illinois regiment of infantry that had marched out to camp, to lead the CAVALRY to the head-quarters of Gen Rosecrans.

I pause here to notice a statement which has been made, that those who went with Col. Woods did not comprise *all* the mutineers. I have my own knowledge to the contrary; and in addition have the statement of Col. W. himself to the effect that he believed not a man was left in camp except those whose duty it was to remain. If any but these did remain, they must have secreted themselves, and there are always some scallawags in the best of regiments.

At or near Lavergne the command was stopped by a heavy force of the enemy's cavalry, under Wheeler, who was destroying wagon-trains, &c. Col. Woods, having had no experience with cavalry, transferred the command to a cavalry officer who had accompanied him. An attack was about to be made, when an escaped prisoner—an officer—came up and reported the rebels to be in overwhelming force. It was therefore not deemed prudent to attack; but the men urged to be led on, saying that annihilation was better than returning to camp. The officer in command afterwards said that it was harder to keep them from sacrificing themselves unnecessarily than it had been to start them from camp. The party then fell back, about a hundred of them going into camp six miles from Nashville, whence they made their way next day to the army; but the majority, disheartened and desperate, having no subsistence for themselves or their horses, and no shelter from the storm that was then raging, returned again to the camp at Nashville, where they hoped to find relief. The horses were so famished that it required skill to mount without upsetting them, and they perished, scores daily, of starvation.

At midnight Col. Woods came again to the camp, with orders to take the command once more to the front; but it was impossible to get a single man out of his blanket. And if it had been possible, the chances were that the trooper would have found his horse dead. This was the last attempt made by Gen. Mitchell to get the CAVALRY into the field. On the evening of next day—the last day of the year—he sent troops and wagons from the city, and the mutineers, by orders, piled their arms and accoutrements into the wagons, and marched to the city Workhouse escorted by the troops.

I encamped my guard and sick on a hillock near the waterworks, formed of offal and the refuse of camps, having been ordered. there as it was an unoccupied point in the defences. It hardly needed military occupation, we thought, for it possessed in itself a *strong* element of defence. The camp here was so aptly named that it must ever remain one of the classic remembrances of the regiment.

On the 1st, 2d, and 3d of January, 1863, those who had gone into the fight returned in detachments. They had seen a week's hard service; both men and horses were nearly used up. True to the determination which they had formed with their comrades, to compel a reorganization of the regiment, a great many of these returned men courageously gave up their arms and joined their comrades in the Workhouse. The latter was consequently overflowed and many were placed without shelter in the yard of the prison. Those who remained in camp had but little shelter nor provisions, the camp equipage having been taken by the Government, and it being impossible to obtain approval for requisitions. The officers positively refused to receipt for any stores that might be drawn for the use of their men. Many of the latter had been stripped of their clothing by the rebels, and were almost naked. I was compelled to assume the responsibility of drawing clothing and issuing it in person to these men in order to save them from freezing to death. Those familiar with the customs of service will understand the great irregularity of this proceeding, and my only excuse is that, though it was irregular, it saved some valuable lives.

I know not how to express my thanks to A. Q. Masters Chas. II. Irwin and T. R. Dudley, to whose kindness I was in a great measure indebted for the ability to draw as stated.

From the first intimation of the troubles, and the purpose to openly demand a remedy, many of the men had received encouragement from their families and friends at home ; and as many of them were connected with influential circles, the promises of legal and other aid carried great weight. But now that the stand had been made, and the strong hand of military power was laid upon those who had taken part in it, none of the promised help from home appeared. On the contrary the journals there teemed with editorials, letters, and despatches, pronouncing eternal infamy upon the mutineers. Their motives were misrepresented or misunderstood, some ascribing it wholly to disappointment in not finding the regiment accepted by Gen. Rosecrans as a "body-guard;" some to the fact of the brigading; some to a desire to escape the service altogether ; and some to the Emancipation Proclamation. This last, it seems, was the impression received at Washington, and by the Secretary of War, who was reported as saying that the outbreak of the regiment from such a motive was the worst thing that had happened during the war. He also sent an inspecting officer to look into the matter, and this officer had evidently received his instructions under the impression I have stated. The Nashville rebels also held the opinion that such was the cause of the trouble, and no doubt wrote astonishing letters to their Confederate friends about the wholesale throwing down of arms by Yankee troops because they were not willing to have the niggers set free. Not a few little dinners were given by rebel admirers to some of these supposed enemies of emancipation. To those who asked advice in the premises, instructions were given to obey St Paul's injunction: " Eat, and ask no questions, for the stomach's sake."

Meanwhile the abuse of the unfortunate men by the organs of opinion at home continued to increase if possible, and scarcely a voice was lifted up to soften or explain their offence. I am tempted to say much more on this point but must hurry on.

Receiving such unbounded censure instead of the advice and assistance that had been promised, finding their motives wholly misunderstood or wilfully perverted, served only to intensify the devotion of the men to their cause. They demanded a trial by court-martial. The majority became mono-manias on this subject, insisting on a court-martial even if it resulted in the death of some of them. Misunderstanding the nature of such a court (which considers *facts*, not *motives*) they hoped that their good intentions might thus be proved to the world. This demand became at last so earnest and obstinate, that it was captiously charged to a desire of escaping service entirely.

This slander is hardly worth disproving; but the facts are at hand, and may as well be stated. It having been reported that an order was extant, allowing men to be transferred from the army to the gun-boat service, a committee of the men in the Workhouse waited upon me with an urgent request that I would ascertain if they could be so transferred; but from officers of gun-boats then at Nashville I learned that there was no such order. And here is an individual instance, still more significant. Among the many whom I removed from the Workhouse to the hospital was one who protested to the last that he would not go, as he had learned that it was the intention of his friends to *purchase his discharge.* I respected his motive, and it was only when the responsibility of his death was thrown upon me by a surgeon's certificate that his life was in danger, that I at last removed him to a hospital.

I may state, too, that with most of those whom I sent to the hospitals, I had difficulty to get their consent, as they looked upon it as deserting the rest.

What better proof can there be that the object of these men was not to leave the service, but to obtain an organization that would result in something better than "temporary arrangements" and disorder?

The Workhouse, where the majority of the men were confined, was a long, low, brick shed, on the river bluff, with a leaky roof, and a bare, muddy floor. The heaps of stone, at which petty offences against civil law were wont to be expiated, still remained in the corners, and were now used as depositories for blankets and utensils, or as a lounge of relief from the unhealthy ground. The few fires, of green or wet wood, filled the area with a dense smoke, and from this arose the title which the men always gave to the place, the "Smoke House." It was a sad sight to see these hundreds of young men, with inflamed eyes, violent coughs, and husky voices; faces purple with fever, or haggard with the wasting diseases engendered by the place. Dreadful as this was, however, the unfortunate youths who had been quartered in the prison yard (some distance from the Workhouse) were in far more pitiable plight. Without shelter of any kind, sick, famished, ragged and freezing; deep in water and mud, and in the accumulated filth of their confinement—the scene was one which I have no disposition to dwell upon.

The court martial demanded by the men was granted. Eleven of their number were tried, and it was rumored had been condemned to death; but no such result was ever published in orders. There was a far more probable rumor to the effect that no formal sentence was ever fixed, the evidence pointing conclusively to the fact that the men had used every means in their power to obtain a proper organization. Of course the truth of the matter can only be known by examining the records of the War Department. On or about the 20th January, Gen. Rosecrans sent a proposition to the confined men, promising to have them speedily reorganized and put into service if they would at once return to duty. Part of them accepted at once, and were quartered in the building that then stood at the corner of Broad and Cherry Sts. The number increased rapidly from day to day, until two other buildings were taken to accommodate them. By the 13th February all had left the prison and the Smoke House. From this time the condition of the men in every way began to improve; and when Colonel Palmer arrived soon after, and began to reconstruct the ruins of the "temporary arrangement" by accepting the resignations of all the officers, the men eagerly went down to the new camp at Murfreesboro as fast as they were sent for. At the same time, on official notice being given, most of those who had in disgust made their way home, returned to the regiment. In less than two months the command was in the field again, sadly thinned, it is true, but fully officered and equipped, and immediately entered upon that career of independent service which needs no further mention here.

In closing, I repeat that I make no apology for the mutiny. I always censured the action of the men as imprudent and untimely, but have always felt that their *motive* merited some public defence. If this plain statement shall dislodge a single prejudice against those in whose interest I have written, they and I will be amply repaid.

Yours truly,

GEO. S. FOBES,

Late Quartermaster of the Anderson Cavalry.

www.ingramcontent.com/pod-product-compliance
Lightning Source LLC
Chambersburg PA
CBHW020809020726
47495CB00008B/2643